MW00990500

THERE IS ONLY US

Stories by
Zoe Ballering

2022 Winner, Katherine Anne Porter Prize in Short Fiction

University of North Texas Press
Denton, Texas

The Year of Perfect Happiness by Becky Adnot-Haynes
Matt Bell, Judge

Last Words of the Holy Ghost by Matt Cashion
Lee K. Abbott, Judge

The Expense of a View by Polly Buckingham
Chris Offutt, Final Judge

ActivAmerica by Meagan Cass
Claire Vaye Watkins, Final Judge

Quantum Convention by Eric Schlich
Dolan Morgan, Final Judge

Orders of Protection by Jenn Hollmeyer
Colin Winnette, Final Judge

Some People Let You Down by Mike Alberti
Zach VandeZande, Final Judge

They Kept Running by Michelle Ross
Polly Buckingham, Final Judge

Printed in the United States of America.

10 9 8 7 6 5 4 3 2 1

Permissions:
University of North Texas Press
1155 Union Circle #311336
Denton, TX 76203-5017

The paper used in this book meets the minimum requirements of the American National Standard for Permanence of Paper for Printed Library Materials, z39.48.1984. Binding materials have been chosen for durability.

Library of Congress Cataloging-in-Publication Data

Names: Ballering, Zoe, 1990- author.
Title: There is only us / stories by Zoe Ballering.
Other titles: Katherine Anne Porter Prize in Short Fiction series ; no. 21.

Description: Denton : University of North Texas Press, [2022] |
    Series: Number 21 in the Katherine Anne Porter Prize in Short Fiction
    Series Identifiers: LCCN 2022024386 (print) | LCCN 2022024387 (ebook) |
    ISBN 9781574418804 (cloth) | ISBN 9781574418866 (ebook)
Subjects: LCSH: Loneliness--Fiction. | Belonging (Social psychology)--Fiction. |
    Self-consciousness (Awareness)--Fiction. | Interpersonal relations--Fiction. |
    BISAC: FICTION / Short Stories (single author) | LCGFT: Short stories.
Classification: LCC PS3602.A62187 T47 2022 (print) | LCC PS3602.A62187
    (ebook) | DDC 813/.6--dc23/eng/20220617
LC record available at https://lccn.loc.gov/2022024386
LC ebook record available at https://lccn.loc.gov/2022024387

ISBN 978-1-57441-880-4 (cloth)
ISBN 978-1-57441-886-6 (ebook)

There Is Only Us is Number 21 in the Katherine Anne Porter Prize in Short Fiction Series

This is a work of fiction. Any resemblance to actual events or establishments or to persons living or dead is unintentional.

The electronic edition of this book was made possible by the support of the Vick Family Foundation.

For my mother, who saved my world from being washed away.

CONTENTS

Ark

On the 152nd day, after a spate of double-crowing at the crack of dawn, Naamah appeared in my doorway. Although she was a normal-sized woman, I had a shoebox-sized cabin, the smallest among any of the handlers, and I had the sense that if she took another step her bulk would pop me out into the passageway. Rain caught at the ends of her eyelashes. Her hair frizzled. She looked mad as a wet hen, which would have solved the chicken fiasco, but she remained defiantly human.

"Karis?" she asked in a tight little voice. Naamah was Noah's wife and first lieutenant. She prowled the decks from gray dawn to gray dusk, soaked from her rounds and reliably ill-tempered. The ark carried eight Covenants— Noah, Naamah, three sons, and three wives—and five handlers tasked with overseeing each of the main animal groups. I was in charge of caring for the birds, and there were handlers for mammals, amphibians, invertebrates, and reptiles. There was no one for fish, because the fish were doing fine without our help. And even though we advised the Covenants on how to properly care for all of the animals, Naamah bore us a special hatred. If God ever gifted her the right to conduct a secondary selection, she would bag us up and toss us overboard in the time it took for the rain to fill a thimble.

"Is something wrong, Matriarch Naamah?" It was the honorific she preferred, a means of reminding us that she would become the progenitrix of the whole human race after God finished drowning the world. I suspected she hated the handlers because we threatened the purity of that line. Nothing would make Naamah madder than if Eliph from Invertebrates had a fling with Tersa from Reptiles and they produced an entire second lineage, so that the children of the Covenant would be forced to share the earth with a bunch of accidental boat babies. According to Noah, God had forbidden copulation during the flood, and the punishment for breaking His commandment was expulsion from the ark and the subsequent extinction of the species. So far the animals had listened, even the rabbits and a particularly randy donkey that had a reputation in antediluvian times for his readiness to stud. But humans were different—we could recognize a bluff.

"Have you checked the chickens recently?" demanded Naamah.

I'd coaxed the eastern rosella to take a nut from between my teeth, I'd petted a collared dove that cooed when I rubbed the slippery feathers at the base of her neck, and I'd taught a rose-ringed parakeet to curse the downpour in language so colorful that it surpassed her plumage. In short, I had really worked my keister off, but I had not checked the chickens, no.

"Have you noticed—" began Naamah, and then the world really turned against me, what was left of it, anyway, because at that moment the two roosters crowed at the exact same time. I could almost have convinced myself that it was one rooster really cockadoodling his delight in life, but then they crowed again in quick succession—two separate, overlapping notes—and it became impossible to deny that there were two of them.

There was nothing to say. I followed Naamah out of my cabin. Everything smelled briny, dirty, dingy, full of dung. We passed the two large avian compartments that housed most of the birds, though I had chosen to cage some of the more aggressive raptors. I'll give it to God— He had really struck fear into their fluttery avian hearts, and in addition to copulation, grounds for expulsion included feeding on one's fellow animals. Still, I could never quite be sure. Sometimes the Cooper's Hawks got a look in their eyes like they were willing to forfeit all future generations for the pleasure of ripping out a pigeon's gizzard.

But the other birds—the ones who ate grasshoppers and walked on lily pads and built blue bowers to woo a mate, the ones who snuck their eggs into other birds' nests and balanced on a single leg above the swirl of water—those birds sang.

"What a racket," muttered Naamah, wrinkling her nose. They clucked and cooed and tweeted and shrieked and drummed their bills and clacked their beaks and the blue jays made a sound like a rusty gate swinging open. I suppose she had a point. Not every utterance could technically be called a song, but I still counted it—they sang for me, an act of celebration. I thought of my mom and how her flock of chickens always clucked when she came near, a deep and satisfied burble. Once I found her in the kitchen feeding sugar water to a weak chick. She held the spoon; he dipped his beak and drank. He had black feathers and shiny black eyes and he cheeped for his mother in the yard. "Very nice, very sticky on your beak," my mother murmured. She taught me this—to always answer. So I sang too, a slurry of nonsense and liquid notes to greet the birds that I had chosen.

My cabin was so far from Noah's state room that we walked for twenty minutes before Naamah led me topsides at the stern. It was 7 a.m., the Open Air Hour for Reptiles, so snakes, crocodiles, turtles, and lizards lay strewn across the deck, attempting to warm themselves in the nonexistent sun. I spied Tersa sitting on a deckbox feeding a pair of blue-tongued skinks a scrap of dehydrated apple. I met her eyes and shrugged, trying to convey the dubiousness of the case against me, though in truth I worried that Noah might treat the rooster debacle as an expulsive offense.

I liked Tersa, but I detested snakes. My heart pounded as I walked past a clump of them, some drab, some jeweled, sliding their smooth, scaled bodies across the smooth, scaled bodies of their fellow snakes. The chill made the reptiles sluggish, and several times Naamah nearly crushed one of the smaller lizards beneath the heel of her rain boot. She didn't seem worried, though. If she flattened the last remaining female blue anole she'd find a way to blame Tersa. Sometimes I suspected that the Covenants had brought us on to fill the quota for that final, most essential species: scapegoats. So great was our value that Noah had selected five instead of two.

Noah's state room had a full bank of windows. He was standing when I arrived, gazing out at the invisible seam where the sky, undifferentiated, met the ocean. He had started shaving his head at the beginning of the flood, and his scraped pink skin reminded me of the turkey vultures in the avian compartment. On the ark they subsisted on a diet of fish and pumpkin, but in non-flood times their bald heads kept them from dirtying their feathers as they feasted on rotting flesh. It pleased me to imagine that Noah followed the same laws of hygiene.

"The Patriarch will see you now," said Naamah before she retired from the room.

Noah turned. His eyes passed up and down my body.

"Sit," commanded Noah. I sat in a chair pulled up across from his desk. He was silent, glowering. I was silent, studying the room. Twenty of my shoebox-cabins could have fit inside. He was trying to convey a level of austerity appropriate to God's most devoted servant, but certain details gleamed luxuriantly. A Cross pen shone on the raw wood of his desk; the claw foot of a bathtub peeked out from behind a curtain.

"First, Karis, I want to express how much I appreciate the work you did while my sons and I were readying the ark. You were instrumental in bringing on the birds. That being said, I think we both know that my family is capable of caring for the animals ourselves. Ham and his wife could handle your job quite easily, maybe even split their time between Reptiles and Birds. So you might be asking yourself, 'Why have God and Noah blessed me with a spot on the ark?' Before we talk about the issue with the roosters—a very serious issue, I might add—I want you to understand that I brought you on as a favor to your mother."

I caught myself midway through the act of rolling my eyes, right when I was looking up at the overhead compartment, and then I lowered my gaze and pretended to fan myself, hoping that Noah might believe that my immense gratefulness had almost made me faint. It's true that my mother is Noah's first cousin once removed, making me Noah's second cousin, making me also distantly related to the other handlers in some complex way I can't remember. But Noah has never acted altruistically; he has never acted for the sake of anyone but God. The birds might be tractable and eager to survive the flood, but they still needed someone sensible to care for them, not that hamhead Ham, or Shem, whom I had once caught licking a banana slug in the Invertebrate compartment, or Japheth, who looked like what would happen if God breathed the breath of life into a potato.

No—Noah picked me because I had a bachelor's in wildlife biology and because, unlike my cousin Hiram, who holds a PhD in avian management and conservation, I had agreed to host the tapeworm. Hiram responded squeamishly when Noah raised the possibility of a human custodian serving as a secondary ark. I was more open to the idea. It seemed like a pretty good deal—tapeworms contain both male and female reproductive organs, which meant I only had to carry one.

"Karis, tell me honestly—did you even try to verify the sex?"

"I did! Patriarch Noah, I swear I did."

How to explain? All those birds luxuriating, squawking, promenading, trying to show themselves off, and me with the power to grant passage. God had ordered them to assemble in the fields around my mother's house, and I was given five days to pick the most ark-worthy pairs. My mom was packing up while I was conducting the selection, and every time I came inside, the house looked a little barer. And I remember feeling guilty because it was Hiram, not me, who would help her move to higher ground.

At dinner each night before I left she asked about the birds, and while I described them she closed her eyes and gave a hum of satisfaction. I didn't always want to talk—it was hard work searching for white ibises with the bluest eyes and peep wrens with the brightest spots—but I tried to stay upbeat to please my mother.

On the morning the ark was scheduled to depart, my mom asked about the chickens. It was an innocent question—she wanted to know what breed I had chosen, because she hated those poofy-headed ones that other people seemed to like. And sitting there, with a spoonful of muesli halfway to my mouth, I felt my heart sink into my rainboots.

In truth, I'd been so caught up by the exotics that I'd barely paid attention to the ordinary species. The previous afternoon, after a final, frenzied selection, I'd sent the remaining birds home and they'd flown and hopped and harrumphed away—including all of the chickens.

"Oh, Karis," said my mother. It was the phrase I dreaded most in all the world.

Of course she let me take her chickens. She wanted to keep the hens for their eggs and the rooster for breeding, but she let me choose two hatchlings from her flock. I *did* check. I tried the venting method, the one where you squeeze the feces out of a chick and then inspect the open anal vent for an "eminence"—a pimple-sized bump that indicates a male. I determined that I had one male and one female chick. Admittedly, I read all this in my mother's poultry manual five minutes before I gave it a try. Admittedly, it did not work out.

"And you never noticed in the past, oh, one hundred days or so, that you had two coxcombed roosters wandering around?" asked Noah.

"Well, you can't really tell the difference between a male and female till the two-month mark, and I've seen the adolescent rooster quite a lot lately, but I never saw both roosters at the same time. And then of course they don't start cockadoodling till five months and I just assumed that all was well until Naamah pointed out the double-crowing."

Noah pounded his fist on the table. The Cross pen jumped like a gleaming silver fish.

"Do you understand," demanded Noah, "that you may wind up responsible for an extinction event?"

"Patriarch Noah," I said in my quietest, most feminine voice, him being very into these types of distinctions, "I think this apocalypse scenario is a little overblown."

At which point I thought he might pick up the Cross pen and stab me in the throat. He intoned the Word of God: "And every living substance was destroyed which was upon the face of the ground, both man, and cattle, and the creeping things, and the fowl of the heaven; and they were destroyed from the earth: and Noah only remained alive, and they that were with him in the ark."

Whenever he quoted God he got that voice people use when they read poetry, quivery and overdramatic. I couldn't say what I was thinking, which was, hold on, old man, calm down. Noah has always been a blowhard. Whenever he tells a story, you must prepare yourself to divide everything in half. If he says he caught a ten-pound tilapia in the Sea of Galilee, you have to assume it was a five-pounder that he pulled from a tank. If he tells you that his grandfather lived for 969 years, it was more like

450. If he says God is so wrathful that He's going to wash corruption off the face of the earth, you have to figure that God is ticked off and sending a moderate deluge.

But there was still this niggling voice in the back of my head. Plenty will remain after all this rain, but did I really have faith in the chickens? They're like feather-covered footballs with dumb, sparkly eyes. I doubted they had the sense to survive a once-in-a-millennium flood. Suddenly I imagined all of my cousins eating quail egg omelets at a family reunion and yelling "Chicken extinctor!" as I tried to hide beneath a table. And I thought about the language that would go extinct or, even worse, would continue on without a referent, so that no one would remember exactly what it meant to chicken out, or to run around like a chicken with its head cut off, or to choke the chicken, though I honestly wouldn't miss that last one.

I panicked just a tiny bit and my mind raced like the female gazelle that used to gallop across the deck. Then one day she slipped and broke through the lifelines and fell overboard. That, too, was almost an extinction event, but Ophir managed to fish her from the water.

Oh God, I thought, what would my mother think? It was her cockerel that I'd mistaken for a pullet. She'd loved birds my entire growing up, always kept chickens, always given them fanciful names. She was the reason I'd majored in wildlife biology with a special focus in ornithology.

She'd even encouraged me to apply for a spot on the ark. My day-to-day duties mostly involved mucking the avian compartment and scrubbing guano off the deck, but my official job title—Diluvial Bird Handler—conveyed a high level of prestige.

The truth, of course, was that I didn't have much skill as an ornithologist. I lived at home and worked as a waitress after I got my degree. Every few months I'd shoot off an anemic application to an avian preserve, halfway wanting it, halfway not. I liked the tips. I liked being on my feet. I liked going home and not worrying about the harm that chewing lice caused to birds with damaged bills. I had no ambition other than to make ends meet. I even liked how it sounded, that phrase. Making ends meet, taking the tails of my life and lifting them up into a smooth little circle. A modicum of success seemed to me like the perfect measure. The only time I ever felt bad was thinking of my mom. She, too, had a smooth little circle of a life. She was a baker and a keeper of birds, and although the smallness of her circle never shamed me, one day I realized that I filled its center completely.

I thought I could bear being called a chicken extinctor for the rest of my life, but I didn't think I could bear for her to hear it. And I thought of my mother high up on the side of Mount Ishtob, and I thought about how much I missed her, and it was at that moment that I formed my plan.

"Patriarch Noah," I said, "My mom has a whole flock of chickens. She took them with her when she and the rest of the settlement evacuated to higher ground. If we could circle back for a quick second, I can dash up the mountain and grab a hen, just to be sure that we can repopulate the earth if God really drowns all the chickens."

"Karis," he said, "when God has finished there will be no seedtime and no harvest, no hot nor cold, no summer nor winter, no day nor night, and no more chickens."

"Right."

"Very well," he grumbled. "God commanded me to save two of every animal, a male and a female, and I shall fulfill God's will. Bring back a hen or you lose your spot on the ark."

Ten days later, we dropped anchor half a mile from Mount Ishtob, and Tersa and Ophir lowered me down on the rowboat.

"You have until nightfall to reverse this extinction event!" screamed Naamah from above. "We'll leave without you if you don't come back in time!"

Either I was anxious or the tapeworm was turning somersaults inside of me. Regardless, I felt ill. I grasped the oars and rowed. I was not, however, a very good rower, having never manned a rowboat in my life, and for a while

I got caught up in the current and drifted farther out to sea than the ark itself.

I glanced at the sky. The clouds made it hard to gauge the time of day, but I guessed I had four hours before sundown. I could hear Naamah shrieking, also the animals making all of their animal sounds.

"Well what do they expect?" I complained to the tapeworm. "I'm not a rower, I'm an ornithologist." I swished my oars through the murky water. Only the sea creatures had flourished in the flood—I imagined fish flippering insensibly beneath me, one world expanding as the other shrank.

Eventually, I righted myself and developed a rhythm, a way of throwing my shoulders into the oars. Naamah's shrieking died away. It took maybe forty minutes to reach the flank of Mount Ishtob. When the boat finally scraped against the shore, it made the sound of pebbles pouring from a pitcher. I was hungry. My stomach and my tapeworm clamored for food. It was that time on the ark when Shem's wife summoned the Covenants and handlers for an afternoon snack—hardtack with a dollop of honey. I thought of my mother waiting at the apex of Mount Ishtob. She didn't have much, but she was still my mother. She always fed me when I came home.

I jumped out and dragged the boat inland, well past the edges of the makeshift beach. I wanted to make sure that the waves couldn't steal it away, because although I didn't believe that God would wipe all life off the face of the earth, the worst-case scenario that Noah had depicted—a chicken-less, Karis-less world—struck me as unspeakably sad. I gazed at the ark. It was long and dark against the gray. I saluted, blew a kiss, made a face, turned my back. I had to bushwhack, but after a while I came to a path I recognized that wound up the side of the mountain.

Was path the right word? Once it had been a hard pack of dirt, but now it channeled excess water. Except that all water had become excessive—it washed over my rain boots in a muddy swirl, moving downward. My mother had lost her home in the first forty days of the flood. The old settlement was somewhere close, east and below, but it unnerved me to see so little debris. I spied a door that had washed up with the skeleton of a dog on top of it, a stroller, a washboard, even, in the midst of ruin, an intact light bulb on a heap of netting. For the most part, though, the world had resolved into water: everything soggy, swallowed, sunk.

The trees that still stood had died in the first rounds of rain. Perhaps they lost their leaves reluctantly, one by one, or all at once in a great denuding. However it happened, those leaves had sunk or disintegrated or swirled into the ocean, so that an angel who only visited the earth in flood would form such false opinions. The angel would believe that trees had no leaves, that gray was the only color, that humans were subordinate to mold. It bloomed all across the land but also up, so that it climbed tree trunks and telephone poles and barbed-wire fences, so dense on the barbs that they became like cotton balls and I could have swabbed my face without a scratch.

I was forced to admit that this was more than a moderate deluge. Not that we were being wiped off the face of the Earth, but that God had decided to make His point more pointed, us heathens being so obtuse.

"God," I cried, looking up at the heavens so that the rain needled into my eyes, "I get your point."

Not that I was planning to stop eating meat or rest on the seventh day, but I promised to be kinder to my mother. She drove me crazy—how she scrunched up her face when she couldn't think of an answer, or half-finished one story and started on another without any indication of the switch. When she cooked she touched every knob, appliance, and serving utensil with soiled fingers, so that after the production of a meatloaf or a pork chop the kitchen looked like a crime scene, and I would follow her huffing with a wet paper towel and take her hands in mine and firmly clean them. I found her even more exasperating than Noah, if I'm being honest, but she was also the person I loved most in the world. Sometimes when I was doing something mindless, lying in bed or scattering birdseed, shame would wash over me, and I would vow to be a better daughter—more loving, more ambitious, more sincere.

The path curved around a patch of bare pines and then the new settlement stretched out before me, a scattering of tiny, tin-roofed cabins. By the quality of the light I guessed I had two hours before sunset. The air was thin here, but thick with rain, and the moisture stuck in my throat like a velvet sock, half soft, half suffocating. Mount Ararat was technically a few hundred cubits taller, but the original settlement had existed at Ishtob's base and no one wanted to schlep to the top of a whole *other* mountain. I could see my mother's cabin down the puddled path. Hers looked just the same as all the others, except for the chicken coop that leaned against its side.

I marched up to her door and knocked and knocked. It occurred to me that she might not be home, and for a moment I felt my heart skitter in my chest. But then— where else could she be? There was nowhere to work, nowhere to walk, and I was sure she was sick of her neighbors. I could feel myself on the edge of tears— that itchy, hysterical feeling that struck me whenever I came home. So I pushed open the door in a fit of panic and there she sat, playing a game of solitaire at her kitchen table.

"Karis," said my mother, so composed that she took another sip from the glass by her elbow. "I thought I imagined the knocking."

"Mom," I said.

"Are you real?"

"Of course I'm real."

"Last week the rain delirium convinced your Uncle Talmin that his drowned dog Dodo had shown up with a tennis ball."

"I brought you a feather," I said. I held out the only gift I had—a green iridescent tail feather that I had plucked from the golden-headed quetzal.

"That is so much better than a tennis ball."

She came around the table and hugged me and I felt how small she was, like a doll with two enormous breasts. I was taller but equally endowed, so that the shelf of her chest ended right below where mine began and we fit together like two buxom pieces of a puzzle.

When I tried to break free, she pushed me away but didn't let go. Her hands clamped down on my shoulders.

"Did Noah kick you off?" she asked in her sternest mother voice.

"It's a long story. I have to get back before sundown."

"Thank God," she said, and we both winced at the phrase. It was one of God's most successful ploys: language so ingrained that it betrayed us into gratitude.

Then she released me, stuck the feather in an empty jar, and puttered around in the kitchen. I sat down at the table. Her cabin was maybe ten by sixteen cubits, with a cooking area in one end and a cot in the other. There were various vessels spaced across the room to catch leaks from the roof. She hadn't brought much in the way of decorations, and I guess as a workaround for loneliness she had started doodling on napkins and taping the napkins to the walls. The one closest to me showed a wiener dog standing on top of an overturned canoe and baying at the sky with a little speech bubble that read, "I miss you, moon."

"Are you hungry, Karis?"

"Yeah, a little bit." I knew I didn't have time to linger, but what I wanted most was for my mom to spoil me like she used to do when I came back from college.

"I'm sorry I don't have anything special to give you. I just used my last tin of meat."

"Aw, too bad," I said. "We're vegetarian on the boat. I guess God forbade us from eating meat. That's what the Covenants say—it's one of the reasons He's supposed to be so mad."

She filled a pot with water, laid a single, speckled egg inside, and lit the stove. Then she came over and sat across from me. It was such a tiny table that our knees touched.

"You've been okay?" I asked.

"Oh, sure," she said, right as a drop of water plinked into the glass that was sitting on the table. "A lot of solitaire. A lot of solitude. I guess I didn't think it would go on for quite so long."

"No one did. Folks were guessing forty days at first."

"Well, Noah did try to set us straight." We rolled our eyes in unison.

"He's really very pompous," I said.

"All the men in this family. You never even knew Methuselah."

I grinned. Nothing felt better than shit-talking the Patriarchs at my mother's kitchen table. It distracted me from how the Covenants were almost certainly shit-talking me on the ark.

Outside the window, I could perceive a slight change in the quality of light, luminous gray shading towards a greater darkness.

"How are the chickens?" I asked.

"Gone. A few of them drowned. A few of them stopped eating. The rooster got an infection on his comb and died."

I felt like I was about to choke. "But there must be some left," I stammered, and I reached out and took a gulp from her glass of endlessly replenishing water. A black circle Sharpied on the wood marked the place to put it back.

"Just my favorite hen, Mizzy. That's her egg you're about to eat. You remember her, the buff-colored orpington with the—"

"Mom, listen, I know this is a huge favor to ask, but I need to borrow Mizzy till the end of the rain." I explained the chicken-sexing disaster and how Noah claimed he would throw me off the ark, and the more I talked the more my mother seemed to crumple, till she was resting her face in her hands. I knew that I was asking too much—that I was leaving my mom with nothing but a wiener dog baying soundlessly on a scrap of napkin. The Covenants weren't much company, but I had Tersa and Ophir and the other handlers, not to mention ten thousand mating pairs who sang when I passed by. There was no one to sing to my mother. She was alone in a leaky cabin with a passel of irritating neighbors and only the sound of the rain.

"Oh, Karis," she said.

"I can stay if you want," I blurted. I meant it. I would stay, if she asked. "We can forget about the chickens."

She shook her head. "You have to take Mizzy. You have to go back to the ark."

"The birds would be fine without me. Ham's a dummy, but he can keep them alive for a while on his own."

"Karis, I'm asking you to take things seriously, for once. The rain isn't stopping. The water keeps rising. Folks are saying God really means to drown us."

She had started believing her pessimist neighbors, but I knew it didn't make sense. How was it possible? How could God make the world and then just wash it away?

The egg timer beeped and my mom stood up and went to the stove. She returned with the egg, peeled and steaming and slick.

"Eat," she said.

I grabbed a knife and cut the egg down the middle. It fell open on the plate. The yolk looked as orange as the missing sun, nestled tightly in the saucer of the white. It was perfect, creamy and hot, with just a hint of jelly at the center. I handed half to my mother.

"You're sure you'll be okay?" I asked when we had finished eating.

And she smiled at me so that her eyes crinkled and I could see her crow's feet.

"I'm sure," she said. "I gave you life. I can give you Mizzy."

Mizzy was so used to being touched that my mom didn't even have to chase her. She just gave her a few caresses and scooped up the hen into her arms. Buff-colored orpingtons are famed for their plumpness, but Mizzy had shrunk and some of her buffness had faded to a sickish cream. She was missing a good chunk of feathers and I could see her goosepimple flesh peeking out, angry and pink, revealing the thinness of her neck.

"Shhh," said my mom as she rubbed Mizzy's head with her thumb. "Mizzy's a good girl."

We were huddled in the covered part of the coop. The floor was a mess of mud and straw. Months of rain had softened the wood so that it felt like standing on a biscuit. My mother showed me how to zip Mizzy up so that her body pressed against my chest and her head stuck out from the top of my raincoat. I supported Mizzy's weight with one arm and hugged my mother with the other—an awkward hug, our shoulders touching and our bellies angled out so that we didn't crush the chicken between us. Our raincoats rubbed together with a plasticky swish.

"Be good, Karis."

"Always."

"Do as Noah asks."

"Most of the time."

"And make sure to eat enough. You look so thin and pale."

I bobbed my head. I had never told my mother about the tapeworm and I never would. I wanted her to keep believing that I had been chosen for the ark because of something exceptional inside of me—something unrelated to the worm.

"I love you," she said. She looked at me with the biggest, saddest eyes. My mom always hated goodbyes.

"I love you," I answered. "And I'll see you on the other side of all this rain."

Then I ran down the hill, following the stream of water and trying not to slip. I dragged the boat into the ever-rising ocean and hopped aboard and rowed like a maniac, till I could make out the corkscrew of Naamah's curls as she marched around keeping order on deck. I had a few minutes to spare before the sun sank below the horizon, and for a moment I just sat there, resting my hands on the oars. I looked down at Mizzy's amber eyes, the flag of her comb like a red flare in the grayness, a sign that the gray had not won. She chortled, then made a sound like a koo koo koo. I revised my estimation of her intellect. She didn't look dumb. She looked infinitely wise, a feathered football with dinosaur feet, having taken the form of a bird to survive that first extinction.

She was, I decided, the most beautiful chicken I had ever seen. I wondered if this was what God intended all along—partial terracide to shift our love to the leftover bits. Maybe He wanted the same: to start again, loving deeply what remained. I thought He was wrong, a big God baby who knocked down the blocks when He noticed an error in the stacking, but I couldn't deny that I felt different now. Once I loved cypresses. Now I poured that love into any tree that still existed. Once I found Gold Laced Wyandottes the most pleasing breed of chicken. Now I loved Mizzy. And my mom, I had always loved her more than all the trees and chickens, but the end of the earth made that clear.

"Is that what you're up to, God?" I demanded, but God, of course, did not answer.

Then Naamah's head poked over the side of the ark, and I raised up the chicken as proof that I had carried out my mission.

"Bring her up," Naamah ordered.

I lashed the rowboat to the lifts and Tersa and Ophir hauled me back aboard the ark. The boat jerked upward. Mizzy clucked and shook her head.

"Wait till you meet the roosters," I whispered to Mizzy, trying to calm her down, and I explained how they show-boated along the taffrail and put the peacocks to shame with their confidence.

The tapeworm twisted in my intestine and Mizzy pressed against my chest. I imagined all my cousins in the gazebo at the family reunion, dragging their forks through piles of scrambled eggs so fluffy they seemed like they might rise up from the plate. Trees rustled above our heads and the poppies bloomed with tissue-paper redness. The sun was shining and the moon would return in the night. Everything gray had come to life and God saw, again, that it was good. Far away, a tame sea broke quietly against the rocks, and the passerines sang from the trees, the thrushes especially for us, song and countersong, a net of notes falling from the sky, but not like rain. I thought of my mother and how everything that was good in me had come from her, and how someday, when we gathered once again, I would not have to hide my face. We would sit side by side at the table, and when my cousins came up to greet us they would call me the Savior of Chickens, and my mother's cheeks would pink with the pleasure of my name.

&

"When Sean McCarthy heads into space, he will leave behind a copy of himself—his identical twin brother, Charlie, a fellow astronaut. Because the McCarthys have virtually the same genetic material, NASA can study how extended time on the International Space Station (ISS) affects the mind and body, using Charlie as the baseline measure." —NASA Press Release

Before the car arrives to pick us up, Enna opens the blue velvet box and selects the medals to pin on my chest. She is very particular about the pinning— she knows, for example, that the stems of the two bronze oak leaf clusters on my Service Medal are supposed to point right, in towards my body, not out to the left as if they were pointing at the world.

"I'm glad you're here," I say. Two days ago we dropped off our son at my mom's house and drove in from Manassas Park, but my brother had a longer journey. Sean is in the adjoining suite right now, pinning his medals alone. He flew first-class from Houston. I can hear him humming through the walls, something jaunty and tuneless, just like him. I have always been the better hummer.

"The baseline brother," says my wife, and she nuzzles her nose against my ear like she is the hummingbird and I am the flower. I find her nose delightfully substantial, not like that ski jump on Sean's wife, which is so skimpy it gets lost between her eyes.

"Baseline: a minimum point used for comparison."

"Oh, stop," says Enna. Now her nose seems to nip instead of nuzzle. "You're cherry-picking to make yourself look bad."

"That's the opposite of cherry-picking. You choose the best things when you cherry-pick."

"You wouldn't know how to choose the best thing if it hit you in the face."

"I chose you."

"Hmmm," she says, a long, husky sigh that I recognize from lovemaking, after we are finished and spooning in bed and she breathes her contentment on the back of my neck. "You're conveniently forgetting the full definition. Baseline: a minimum or starting point used for comparison. You're a starting point, Charlie. You're like the first letter in the alphabet."

"I'm an A?"

"You're an alpha."

I clack my teeth like I intend to nibble her.

"You're full of shit."

"My baseline lover," she murmurs, and right at that moment my brother walks in and the door becomes a mirror that holds my body. We are burly, well-decorated, and so thoroughly bald that the same blue vein oxbows above our left ears.

"Sorry," he says. "I forget my manners when Virginia's not around. The front desk just called to say the car is here."

Enna grabs her purse and I pull on my coat. Before we leave, Enna inspects Sean's uniform and tut tut tuts.

"You shouldn't need a wife to get this right," she says, repinning his Service Medal so that the stems point in towards his heart. He has four clusters; I have two.

"Alpha," I exhale as we wait for the elevator to take us down.

"Did you say something?" asks Sean.

I don't answer. I take my wife's hand and start humming the chorus to "Sweet Caroline." The doors ping open and we crowd inside.

Outside of the auditorium, an easel displays a promotional image that the publicity department shot the day before. Sean and I face each other in profile. My brother wears his full biosuit. The immaculate bubble of his visor curves into the space between us. I am wearing a thin white T-shirt, as if I intend to spend Sean's year in space lounging on my couch eating crinkle-cut potato chips. I would have preferred a tracksuit or a blazer—anything, really, to suggest that my life will continue on earth.

"You both look so serious," says my wife. In the image, we glower at each other. We are standing two feet apart, so that if I extended my arms I could touch Sean in his most ticklish location, brush the tips of my fingers down his throat.

"At least they made it easy to tell us apart," I mutter.

The photo reminds me of the baby album at my mom's house, the one where she spelled our names on the cover with adhesive foam letters. It would have made more sense to affix the letters to our foreheads—we are indistinguishable in all photos up until the age of eight or nine, at which point Sean started growing out his hair. When my son pages through the album, he points at every picture and asks, "Is that you or Uncle Sean?" and every time I answer, "That is me."

Our mother never asks. She believes that motherhood has bestowed on her a special power. If the baby is smiling or its eyes look exceptionally blue or it is lifting something, even something paltry like a plastic rattle, she says, "That's Sean." But if the baby appears ill or has a rash on its chest or is lying bare-butted on a blanket, she says, "That's your butt. I'm sure that's a picture of you."

"Mom," I say, "our butts look exactly the same."

"A mother always knows," she answers.

My wife is not so confident. Perhaps she remembers the time she goosed Sean by accident at a cocktail party. Instead she coos at every single image of a baby, including a rogue photo of our cousin Johnny that somehow got slipped into the back. He looks nothing like us, born with a full head of black hair. "What a cutie," she says. "That must be you."

But my wife has finally learned to tell our butts apart—she pats me discreetly before she peels off into the auditorium. Our handler leads us backstage, where we sit side by side as a makeup artist works on our faces. I can hear the host trying to rev up the audience, scientists in dress slacks who clap so sedately that it sounds like a gentle, cleansing rain. In the midst of being bronzed, Sean reaches out to touch me. He can't turn his head, so his arm swats at the air before he finds my shoulder.

Then they are rushing us onstage. We sit in boxy white chairs, half-facing the audience, half-facing the host. I can see my wife in the front row, beaming. Her big nose shines.

After we've talked through the mission plan, the host, a jovial ex-newscaster with alarmingly white teeth, steeples his fingers underneath his chin. His eyes twinkle as he stalks the TV moment.

"Now that we've gotten through the science stuff, I think we all want to hear about your relationship."

Sean leans forward, smirking. I steel myself to launch into the script.

"Well, at the end of this mission I'll have 540 total days in space and Cherry's spent what, fifty-three, fifty-four—"

I hate it when he uses my nickname in front of people we don't know.

"Fifty-five days, thank you very much."

"So basically I do everything better than him."

"He's actually worse at everything," I say.

Sean turns to face the audience full on.

"Whoa, little bro, don't get cocky. I was born six minutes earlier, so I'm a little bit wiser—I've spent a little bit longer on earth."

"If wisdom equals earth time, you're about to lose a year."

"Sure, Cherry. Earth wisdom is good and all, but space—" I imagine the cameras zooming in on his face as he works up to his reverie. "Space is different. In space you look down at that little blue marble and you gain insight into the nature of the universe, how finite and precious our world is. Brother, am I right?"

I remember the blue curve falling away beneath my feet. Clouds swirled across the water like cream. We were moving so fast on the Space Station that we could watch night fall before us, endless beads of light coming into being as billions of people defeated the dark. As children we kept marbles—puries, clam broths, and onionskins—but we never owned a marble that could equal earth.

"He's right," I say, meeting Enna's eyes. "Space teaches something different."

I can see my son through the living room door while Sean and I sip beers in the kitchen. Theo is playing a video game, bobbing and weaving as he strafes zombies or mutants or mole people, whatever bad guys are currently in vogue. I wish that he would learn to keep his cool. When you go up in a Soyuz and everything is shaking and you feel like the metal might peel back and let your whole body burn in an instant, you still have to page through the flight plan and pretend you aren't praying for your life.

"I have to put him to bed soon," I say softly.

"I can do it," says Sean. "Uncle Sean Special Delivery—I'll just bundle him up, unhook him from that game, and throw him into bed."

"Nah. He's been at Ma's house. I've missed him."

"I could be you. Think he'd notice?"

"I could be you," I say, but we both know it isn't true.

"You know I was joking, right?" There's something anxious crawling on his face. "'I do everything better,' all that stuff on stage. No one cares about astronauts anymore, but sibling rivalry—that story sells. People respond because they know it can't get ugly. They know we're gonna go home, share beers, and reminisce."

He picks up his bottle and tries to toast me, but I do not move to meet him. I parrot the press release instead.

"When Sean McCarthy heads into space, he will leave behind a copy of himself."

"Cherry," he says, "you know I didn't want that. You have to tell a story from a certain point of view, that's all."

I think of the fourth grade, back when Sean and I were on the same Little League team and I had struck out twice the game before. I lay in bed pretending to be sick and Sean pretended to be me. I heard the stories afterwards, the myth of my achievement. My teammates told me that they had never seen me run so fast, kicking my heels up behind me, pounding down the baseline as the ball passed over my head. They watched in wonder as I slid feet first and touched my toe to home. The ump hovered above my stretched-out body, slashing his hands. I was safe. No one flipped me over in the red dirt and declared that his butt was not mine.

"While Charlie McCarthy remains on earth, he will send a copy of himself to space," I murmur.

"That story is just as true," says Sean.

He reaches across the table and places his hand on top of mine. The intimacy of the gesture makes me squirm. It is the act of a lover, not a brother. I hope that Theo doesn't turn his head.

"I love you, Cherry," he says.

"I love you, Sean," I answer as I slide my hand away. He is flying home tomorrow. A week back with Virginia and Rigel, and then from Texas to Kazakhstan, a twenty-hour flight. The refrigerator hums into the silence. I give in and clink my beer to his before we take another sip.

The four of us watch from one of the observation rooms at the DC headquarters: wife, son, nephew, brother. Virginia is staying in our guest room and Rigel is sleeping in the trundle that pulls out from Theo's bed. Enna decided not to attend. It was still dark outside when she went to work—a twelve-hour shift at the Prince William ER.

"Your brother is going to be fine," she said, kissing me on the cheek while I tried to burrow underneath my pillow.

The video link shows the Baikonur Cosmodrome in Kazakhstan. The Soyuz rocket on the screen has a syringe-like quality. Six hours after takeoff and the needle tip of its docking mechanism will slide into the corresponding port on the ISS. It points upward on the launch pad, ready to pierce the sky. Sean appeared on the screen twenty minutes ago and we said our goodbyes, waving fiercely, full of false cheer. Now Virginia is sitting at the conference table twisting a bangle on her wrist. My son and nephew are drawing on the whiteboard with fat blue markers—an eight-legged crab-thing chasing a man whose limbs seem to bend like spaghetti.

"No," says Rigel, erasing Theo's attempt at teeth and instead drawing fangs. "It's a *man-eating* crab." Theo is eight months older and a little taller, though I don't have faith that the difference will continue on in my family's favor. He stands beside his cousin, adding a speech bubble to the spaghetti man. I pray he doesn't write something inauspicious like, "I'm about to die!"

Theo pauses, holding the marker so that the tip nearly touches the board.

"Dad," he says, "what's it like?"

"What's what like?"

"Seeing the earth."

It was something he used to ask about all the time before I tucked him into bed. I would spin such stories: sunrise calling into being the brightest blue, how the rivers run like necklaces across the earth.

"You've heard me talk about it before. There's even a term for it—the Overview Effect. Suddenly you look down and you realize that everything that has ever been, everything that you have ever loved, is down there on that fragile blue ball."

"It's time," calls Virginia. The readout on the screen has ticked down to sixty seconds. The boys cap their pens and take their seats between us. The spaghetti man's speech bubble stays blank—I fill it with a prayer. Last month, a faulty sensor caused a Soyuz to spin out of control thirty miles above the earth. The astronauts escaped by performing an emergency separation, but I wish that Enna were here to hold my hand.

Virginia flips the audio switch and we can hear the NASA announcer overlaid across the Russian commands.

"The second umbilical now separating from the tower, marking less than fifteen seconds, the engines igniting—"

The whole column turns orange and the burned propellant piles up on the launchpad like tulle. For a moment all I can see is the silver needle ascending. Then the screen flashes white and the rocket rises into clean air. The video renders the burn of the propulsion as a six-sided star. If we were there, it would be too bright to watch.

"Is it okay?" asks Rigel.

"So far so good," I say. "The first few minutes are the riskiest."

The video switches to the inside of the Soyuz. Sean, the commander, is sitting in the middle between two flight engineers. He can't reach the control panel because he's belted in, so instead he uses a pointer tipped with a soft rubber nipple that allows him to press the necessary buttons. He once referred to it in an interview as his fancy stick. That's how I see it—the scepter he carries into space. He glances up at the camera and grins. He looks calm. Maybe it's actual; maybe he's acting. The strain never shows on his face.

"Flying true and nominal," he says. I recognize the incantation. I have spoken it before.

"He's telling us that all is well," I say.

That night I dream that I am the spaghetti man, stretching my tubey legs towards safety, tapping my toe against home. When I come awake it is a gentle reentry into consciousness, none of the gasping of a nightmare. Enna, the big spoon, has peeled off and curled herself away from me. I want to stroke her back. I don't. Instead, I sit on the edge of the bed, adjusting my bare feet to the coolness of the floorboards. Then I stand and pull on my sweatshirt and wander down the hall to check on Rigel and Theo. I crack the door and squint my eyes. Two lumps, two leggy bodies under blankets. They are almost indistinguishable, except for the hierarchy of beds—Theo in the twin, Rigel below him in the trundle.

Sean named him Rigel after the blue supernova that forms Orion's foot. It is the brightest star in the constellation, which means that it should have received the designation Alpha Orionosis. Rigel's only competition comes from Betelgeuse, a variable star that dims and brightens over a period of roughly four hundred days. The astronomer John Herschel must have caught Betelgeuse in a period of waxing. He mistook it for the brighter of the two and therefore misassigned the designation.

When I walk out on the porch, I find Virginia sitting on the steps. It is cool, but not too cold, and the crescent moon crowns the cherry tree. The ember of her cigarette burns brighter as she takes a drag.

"Guess Sean can't chastise you for smoking," I say.

"Not for another year."

"I could do it for him."

"Don't bother."

I watch ash stack on the tip. I imagine Sean using the rubber nipple on his fancy stick to knock it loose.

"I'm happy for him," she says. "He tries to explain what it's like, but of course I can't understand. What do I know? The best thing I ever saw was a sunset in Tahiti on our honeymoon."

I crane my head. I can see the stars beyond the eaves.

"What's he doing up there?" she asks.

"It's what, one, one-thirty? They'll spend the next hour matching orbits with the Space Station. Then they'll dock. You can't see much from the Soyuz, but once he's on the ISS he'll have a chance to look down."

"What do we look like, in the dark?"

I shrug. "There are pretty ways of putting it, but sometimes, honestly, it just looks like a really aggressive rash. Like the cities are these glowing red boils."

She laughs.

"Sean never explained it that way, but he would like it."

We sit in silence until she finishes her cigarette. She stubs it out in one of the planters, then picks up the butt and stands up. There's a kind of accidental reverence in the way she cradles it, like she is holding something sacred in her palm.

My second mission came three years after the *Columbia*. Those were the shuttle days—we launched from Florida then. We were delivering supplies to the ISS and testing new equipment designed to keep us from burning up when we came back to Earth. Theo was a baby. I asked Sean to be there with Enna even though he had to leave his newborn son in Texas. I remember kissing Theo's soft bald head as Enna held him, kissing her, clasping Sean. Thirteen days in space. I felt sure I would come back, but just in case—I wanted him to be there with my family.

"Virginia," I call as she retreats into the house. "You know you can come visit any time. Or you can send Rigel for the summer, if you need a break. Theo would like it. It would be like having a brother."

"I appreciate it," she calls back.

I stay on the porch, my hands shoved underneath my sweatshirt. I can see the cool blue of Rigel and the orange of Betelgeuse, which must be waning now—it looks like a sooty smudge beside its brother. For all I know, Sean could be right above, 250 miles distant, as close to here as Yonkers is. Someday, perhaps, he will pass above while we are both asleep and I will dream the myth of stealing home while he is dreaming the memory, two slides of the same image held up to the light so that their edges match. I hope that the scientists who run so many tests will catch this doubling, when the baseline brother dreams the same as the man in space.

Then Sean is gone. He spends a year in space. Coming back is just the plunge through atmosphere. Returning isn't easy, but it's quick.

The night that Sean comes home I dream of a great shaking. The windows turn from pink to red to maroon to black and pieces of the capsule burn away. I dream that the parachute drags us through the grasslands and when we emerge, two women dressed in green and yellow offer us a round of bread with a ramekin of salt lodged in its center. We sit on the ground cross-legged feeling loopy, trying not to vomit as we take a pinch of bread, a pinch of salt.

When they call to say that he has landed safely, I cry in a way that I have never cried before, great ragged sobs that rip me up. We are sitting at the breakfast table. Theo stares as I try to hide my face inside a bowl of cereal.

"Did something happen to Uncle Sean?" he asks.

"No, sweetheart," says Enna. She is drying her hands from washing dishes, long, methodical swipes that extend up to her elbows where the suds have reached. "Your father's crying because Uncle Sean is safe."

Enna sends him from the room. She pulls three unripe avocados from a paper bag and hands me the bag in case I start to hyperventilate.

"Oh, shush," she murmurs, massaging my shoulders. "He's safe, my love. He made it home."

A week later, Sean and his family fly to DC so that we can undergo the full battery of tests. We spend four days performing balloon analogue risk tasks and matrix reasoning, undergoing MRIs and ultrasounds, and peeing into cups. Sean has changed in little ways. He is taller. His skin is so sensitive that I can see where the collar of his shirt rubs a red mark around his neck. When the doctors hand us clipboards full of paperwork, he comes and sits beside me, leaning in so that our shoulders touch, tapping his pen to the parts that he can't read. They believe his vision will fully return in the next few months, but they aren't sure. It's not a secret, nor does he want it to be—on the fourth day we are scheduled for a retinoscopy—but there is something furtive in the way he curls around the clipboard, like a dog that knows it has done a bad thing. I whisper when I read aloud to him.

At the end of the four-day test period, our mother summons us to dinner. We arrive in a rented minivan— two wives, two sons, two brothers—and when she throws open the door I am surprised, as I always am, by how old she looks. I see her more often than Sean, both because I'm earthbound and because she lives in Baltimore, but her hair is threaded grayer, her wrinkles deeper, her eyes more tired and diaphanous, as if the iris itself is fading with age. Cooing commences. Sean gives her a gift that she opens in the living room. It is a matryoshka doll painted with his face and containing, in its belly, five more Seans.

"A gift from the Russians," he says, and she laughs and sets it on the bookshelf.

The boys gravitate towards Elvie, our mother's Pomeranian; they halfway play and halfway persecute, so that I have to shout at them from the kitchen. Sean and I stand beside our mother as she stirs and simmers and seasons. We advise her on how to spice the colcannon potatoes, even though we have no idea. It's really just an excuse to squeeze her shoulder and tease her, to shout our appreciation for everything: our mother, our families, gravity, Guinness, potatoes, the Irish, the earth.

"Oh my boys, my boys," says our mother once we are ready to eat. "I'm so glad you've come home."

She sits at the head of the table and has arranged us as if we are facing off against our archetypes. Me across from Sean, Virginia across from Enna, Theo across from Rigel. Rigel gobbles, but Theo mistrusts the pinkness of the Irish-spiced beef.

"Don't they have salt in space?" asks Enna after Sean picks up our mother's saltshaker, a penguin that seasons from its eyes, and weeps a layer of salt across his plate.

"Salt," he grunts, "but no shaking." And he shovels such a huge lump of beef into his mouth that I have to explain how microgravity makes shaking impossible—the grains might float away and scratch someone's retina or lodge in the ventilator and cause a systems failure.

"We use liquid salt," adds Sean once he has finished chewing.

Rigel's fork screaks across his plate as he corrals his last potatoes. Under the table, Elvie gnaws on a rawhide bone—the only evidence of her industry is the grinding sound that rises from our feet.

"What's wrong?" demands Rigel, who has noticed the beef building up on Theo's plate. "You don't like it?"

"It looks funny," says Theo.

"You look funny," Rigel shoots back.

I remember when Rigel came to visit in July and I took the boys for ice cream. Rigel and I ordered triple chocolate brownie. Theo ordered bubblegum. Then we wandered through Baldwin Park, licking feverishly to fight the sun.

"Bubblegum's a sissy flavor," said Rigel. He would enter sixth grade in September and he had already mastered the art of the middle school insult. But Theo didn't care—the ice cream glowed in his hand like a pink beacon. Chocolate is dour, but bubblegum sheds light.

Rigel had an effective ice cream management plan. Theo did not. He let fat drops fall on his fingers and down his arm and then slurped these up, tenderness enacted on himself. I knew that Enna would laugh at me if I brought home one spotless boy and one soiled one, so finally I insisted that we stop trying to walk and eat. I sat at a picnic table and Theo and Rigel sat on the tabletop, displaying their elaborate sneakers. Rigel had just turned eleven; for the next few months, he and Theo would share that limbo age. They seemed too old to want to impress me, too young to want to impress the girls at school. It must have been a desire to impress the world in general, to arrange the tableau of their Converse zipbacks and their checkered Vans so that passersby would recognize their greatness.

When Rigel had finished his ice cream cone, he pulled out his phone and scrolled through Sean's Twitter feed, narrating each of his father's Tweets. Theo looked on, licking absently.

"Here's the flower he grew in space, the first space flower, and here's where he's juggling the fruit, #zerogravity #spacefruit, and here's where he drew a picture of a candle on a piece of paper and sang me happy birthday and then, when he's done singing and I'm supposed to blow it out, he holds his finger up in front of the orange part to hide the flame. Here's a picture where the sun is rising—"

I counted possible hashtags in my head: #earth-twin #dadbod #taxtime #sciatica #tweenparenting. In November I had poked real candles into a real birthday cake; I had touched the lighter to eleven wicks—real flame that Theo tried to vanquish, blowing so forcefully that he misted his birthday cake with spit.

Now Theo pushes the Irish-spiced beef to the side of his plate so that soft folds of meat hang over the edge and touch the tablecloth. Enna leans over and whispers in his ear.

"Sean, Charlie, you haven't told us how the tests went," says our mother.

"Yeah," chimes in Rigel. "Are you still identical?"

"Pretty much," says Sean. "Just a few little differences." He pauses. He squints at the pattern along the rim of his plate, intricate, interlocking blue lines that he probably perceives as a solid ring.

"He's two inches taller now," I volunteer. "Microgravity elongated his spine."

Our mother claps her hands.

"How wonderful," she says. "We'll have to put it on the wall."

After we finish eating, she makes us go to the living room to the place on the doorframe where we mark our heights on the wall.

I can see our mom's height in green marker from eight years ago. I think she may have shrunk since then, but I don't want to be the one to tell her. I can see our dad's height from the final time before the stroke. I can see our friend Antonio and our Aunt Deirdre and our favorite babysitter, Anne Marie. I can see our sons on the wall and our wives when we added them during a drunken

Christmas party many years ago. I can see when we were toddlers and boys and teenagers and students at the US Naval Test Pilot Academy. We share a line each time. "Charlie & Sean" it reads. Dad always used an ampersand, because an ampersand denotes a greater closeness than "and."

Sean presses himself up against the wall.

"It's gotta be you, little bro," he says. I am the only one tall enough to reach, so I mark his height in Sharpie and I write his name along the newest line.

Theo squeals when Sean steps back. "Uncle Sean was right," he says. "He grew."

"I stretched," says Sean, and I think of our body stretched out and reaching towards home.

Then the boys clamor to update their heights on the wall. After I mark Rigel, Theo slips beneath my hand and takes his place. I can tell that the difference is shrinking and that soon my nephew will overtop my son.

"No cheating," says Enna. She reaches out and lets her hand linger on my shoulder. I look up for a moment, look around the room. All the grownups are smiling, their faces pink from the wine. Out of the corner of my eye I mistake the matryoshka doll for my own face. But who's to say? We do look exceptionally similar. I imagine a matryoshka ad infinitum, stretching out in both directions, so that it becomes impossible to tell who is the seed that started the chain and who is the apex that ended it. It is an act of infinite spooning, spooned safe inside of someone else and spooned around them, so that, in fact, there is never a big spoon or a small spoon, there is only us.

I turn back to my son. My hand looks old to me, more veined than I remember. Theo's hair is messy, curly, brown. I press it flat and mark his height upon the wall.

"How 'bout that, Cherry?" says Sean.

"Sure is something," I answer, looking down.

Substances:
A School Year

September

Every day we met for lunch in the art classroom in the
school's east wing. It was the woodshop before the woodshop closed—a cavernous space full of defanged band
saws and belt sanders stewing in desuetude. The art
teacher, Mr. Devine, had dragged two long tables into the
front of the room. Here, beneath the first bank of fluores-
cent lights, elective-hungry underclassmen swirled leaded
tap water into watercolor paints. The woodshop stretched
out behind them—dark, dusty, dank. During the lunch
hour, Mr. Devine would sit at his computer and exchange
direct messages with his girlfriend, an aesthetician named
Oksana, who lived in Belarus. He left the door of the woodshop unlocked because we were quiet, orderly, and clean,

and because of his fondness for Lisa, an accomplished watercolorist who always asked after Oksana's health.

The far corner of the woodshop contained a set of metal stairs. Rather than connecting us to the endless secretions of the student body, these stairs—our stairs— opened onto a grated landing that served as a storage space for stacks of wooden toasters. The toasters lined the edges of the landing, leaving a small space for the four of us to sit. Diego held the clipboard at the head of the group, and Sayla and Lisa assumed their spots on either side of him. Leopold arrived last because he had fourth period in one of the portable classrooms. He used an anti-bacterial wipe to sanitize as he ascended, then sealed us inside. The toasters were fashioned from cubes of unfin-ished pine, each with two slots, each slot stuffed with a toast-shaped piece of wood. We liked the idea that pine oil was a minor antiseptic. We felt cocooned among the toasters, free of germs.

Lisa had secured the landing at the end of sopho-more year, and now, as newly minted upperclassmen, we debated the nature of the substances as the school envel-oped us again. We didn't care about anything the other students loved: homecoming, house parties, horoscopes, laser shows, lanyards, voting, veganism, volleyball, ESPN, Thespian Club, macro- *or* microeconomics. Only the sub-stances awakened us from our ennui.

"I have another sighting to report," said Sayla as she pried open a segmented Tupperware that kept her celery sticks from mingling with her baby carrots. It was the Friday of our first week back. "A soup-like substance on the floor five tiles to the left of Mr. Zerba's classroom door."

Diego made a notation on the map. "Sighting time and detailed description?"

"Second period. Partial solids. Some thin yellow noodles. Also, carrot chips and three peas, apparently rehydrated."

"You're describing the contents of a Cup of Soup," said Diego.

"Yeah," chimed in Lisa. "Someone must've poured it on the floor."

"That's vomit, Lisa," said Sayla, shaking her head.

"No way," said Lisa. She scrunched her freckled forehead with displeasure. "It's a joke, alright. Like someone saying, 'This is one third of my daily sodium intake, I am basically ingesting a Cup of Salt. This is fit for a floor, not a human body.'"

Leopold, who was currently ingesting a Cup of Salt, set down his spork and turned pink.

Lisa patted him on the leg. "Don't worry," she murmured. "Everything's fine in moderation."

Later, we would issue an injunction against all liquids except for bottled water.

Later, we would forbid unprotected contact, including the patting of legs.

Later, we would ban all forms of hybrid cutlery, because we mistrusted things that occupied the spaces in between—sporks, sleet, stew, prose poems, anadromous fish, adolescents, old people who looked young and young people who looked old, dusk, comatose states, semicolons, speed walking, deciduous conifers, marital separation, jammed elevators, tunics, and tadpoles with legs.

Later, we would strike the word "moderation" from our meeting minutes because we considered it a slur against sterility.

But those were our salad days, September, back when we were young and we did not understand the nature of the substances.

October

We had just settled into our routine—pep rallies in which acned cheerleaders performed thigh stands to thunderous applause, early release on Fridays, a vending machine on the second floor that spit back even the crispest dollar bills—when a truly evil substance tried to ruin us.

Sayla heard about it first. One of the jocks from her third-period civics class burst through the door, the hall pass swinging from his hands.

"Dude," he said, "there's a bloody tampon in the water fountain."

"Someone find Manny!" shouted Mr. Arney, the civics teacher. Manny was the head custodian. He was stocky and hairless and had a deep, gravelly voice that itself seemed like an implement of cleanliness. We imagined him chipping gum off the underside of desks simply through the act of speaking. When faced with any substance, even one that would make us scatter, he would squint, scratch his chin, and eliminate the substance at its source.

In the ensuing pandemonium, as the students groaned and high-fived and Mr. Arney called the office, Sayla slipped away to document the scene. She passed around her phone as we gathered together on the landing.

"That's ketchup," said Lisa, scrolling through the photos. She handed the phone to Diego and then dredged a chicken nugget through the very substance that she had just identified. Later that week, we would issue an injunction against condiments.

"Everything's a joke to you," huffed Sayla.

Lisa bit the nugget neatly in half. "Ketchup," she repeated.

"Right," said Sayla. "Because menstrual blood is ketchup, mold is just green-colored glitter, and even the phlegm we found last week is nothing but the tapioca from a Snack Pack."

"Regardless of the nature of the substance," said Leopold, "it's hard not to feel that this is directed at the two of you." His eyes bounced back and forth between the girls.

"What do you mean?" said Lisa, but we were sure she knew. The other day we had noticed a stash of tampons in her backpack when she was digging around for a pencil. They were individually wrapped in pink plastic and might have been mistaken for some type of specialty candy, but our sophomore health class had taught us all about these things. That particular substance struck adolescent girls earlier and earlier according to our health teacher, Mrs. Horne.

It was statistically likely that both Sayla and Lisa had menstruated for several years, though Sayla insisted that the Great Omnipotent Unpolluted One had delayed the onset of her period. We believed her. We had never noticed any smells or stains or secret stores of feminine hygiene products that would cause us to question her purity.

"We can't fight this evil alone," said Diego, calling us back to the tampon at hand.

But who could help? The other students, perhaps aware of the import of our mission, avoided us when we passed them in the halls. We were glad that our dedication cleared a sterile space around our bodies, but sometimes we felt like there were only four of us in all the world. Other than unlocking the classroom door, Mr. Devine had no time for us. The only substances he cared about were the ones he imagined making with Oksana. When Lisa asked Ms. Deng, the school nurse, about the substances, Ms. Deng took her question as a declaration of substance abuse and sent Sayla home with three brochures. Mrs. Butler, Sayla's college counselor, grumbled about how hard it was to keep the building clean.

"This building was intended as a midsize women's stenography school, and now it holds 1,500 teenage bodies," she said as she closed her office door. Sayla worried that Mrs. Butler had added a demerit to her file—a black mark that oozed across the paper.

"So much for Stanford," said Sayla, who had always struck us as Most Likely to Succeed. "I'll probably end up majoring in business at one of my safety schools, and then I'll graduate with $30,000 in debt and spend the rest of my life as the teller at a credit union, shuffling through other people's grubby bills." Every time she took a bite of baby carrot, she held up the nubby remainder as if she could read her future in the smooth orange flesh.

November

Then one day Leopold was dinking around with a hall pass, killing time before the end of class, and he walked past Manny mopping near a locker at the exact same moment that the locker disgorged a stream of sour milk. Later the story came out that one of the drama kids had left an open carton inside and that a textbook must have fallen over and knocked it loose. But we knew better. Manny and the substances were in cahoots. He didn't clean up, so much as he caressed the messes.

"It's like he knew it was coming," said Leopold. After his encounter with Manny, he returned to fourth period in the portable classrooms, then jogged to reach us when the bell rang. The armpits of his shirt were stained with sweat. We pretended not to notice.

Leopold's story convinced us. No more tapioca truthers. Blood, mud, milk, paint, phlegm, poop, pudding—it was immaterial. Now we understood that while the substances might adopt a certain shade or texture, the school itself secreted them. We imagined Manny dragging his mop back and forth across the floor until the school released that gush of curdled cum.

Both Sayla and Leopold had a free sixth period that they devoted to tracking Manny's movements. They brought back reports of how he sniffed his fingers or ate the snickerdoodle left on a Styrofoam tray that some kid hadn't thrown away or answered his phone in Spanish. "Mi amor," he repeated, "mi amor," and Leopold, who had taken intermediate Spanish, informed us that this meant, "My love, my love."

"He's describing the school," said Sayla. "He's telling someone else about his lover."

All four of us were tracking Manny by November's end. He rubbed mops and brushes and paper towels across the ready flesh of our school, his lover, and we scuttled after him like sterile crabs, crouching next to water fountains, shielding our bodies behind locker doors, and holding up three-ring binders to hide our faces. Mostly, we kept detailed maps of the spots to which he tended to return. These, we surmised, were the pleasure centers through which he stroked the school to a froth of ecstasy. Health class had given us an understanding of the student body, but we did not understand the school. We only knew that if we memorized the tender spots, we might also find the weak spots, the organs of pleasure that could easily shift into organs of pain.

"Leave me alone, you crazy kids!" shouted Manny whenever he saw us in the halls.

December

As the year wound down, we lost our single-minded focus. We exhausted ourselves. The school churned out certain products endlessly: substances, homework, isolation, stress. Our parents told us to start thinking about college, and as we peered into the future, all our careful laws decayed.

Lisa patted Leopold all the time, despite our warnings.

Leopold arrived later and later, and we wondered if he belonged to a competing faction, perhaps a separate quartet devoted to charting the spread of STDs.

Sayla's grades started to slide. She became addicted to hand sanitizer. We wouldn't let her light the Bunsen burners in chemistry class because we worried that the alcohol might ignite her skin.

Diego developed an enormous whitehead on his chin. We pinched our fingers in anticipation.

"Pop me," pleaded the pustule. "Bring forth more substances. Admit that you are us and we are you." But we refused.

On the last day before Winter Break, we selected one of the toasters and placed it at the center of our circle. One by one, we Sharpied a private prayer onto a single piece of toast, then fit the slice back into its slot.

"O Great Omnipotent Unpolluted One," intoned Diego, "give us the strength to defeat the school. May all contaminants burn in the fire of your purity. May sanitizer rinse the sin from our hands. Forgive us our bodies, our weakness, our pubescent imperfection. Each and every day we consecrate ourselves again to You."

Diego pressed the wooden lever and the toast leapt up and clattered cleanly to the floor.

"Amen," we said in unison. We agreed to go home for Winter Break and return with renewed exactitude, fortitude, obedience, loyalty, and vigor.

January

We returned with renewed exactitude, fortitude, obedience, loyalty, and vigor. On our first day back, we experienced five substance-related events, including, most notably, a series of brown clumps near the first-floor lockers. Lisa insisted that the women's soccer team had tracked in mud on their cleats, but Sayla and Leopold identified the brownness as poop.

Even just the possibility of fecal matter marked a major turning point. We decided that the time had come to assemble our materials of war.

Lisa swiped a bunch of jars from her mother's spice rack, dumped the spices in the trash, and started storing samples in a corner of the landing. As soon as she received word of a possible substance, she finagled a hall pass and appeared on the scene with a pair of tweezers. Flakes of ketchup-blood with a dusting of nutmeg. A scoop of tapioca-phlegm in a jar that still smelled like freeze-dried shallots. A smear of mud-poop with the last pinch of paprika.

Sayla had a knack for thievery and stole, in the course of one week, three boxes of latex gloves from Ms. Deng, four pairs of plastic safety goggles from the chemistry lab, and a stack of surgical masks from the hospital where her grandmother was currently succumbing to a different set of substances.

Leopold brought the shower liners from his step-mom's house so that we could make protective suits. We had him lie down on one of the liners, and then Lisa traced the outline of his body with a Sharpie, lingering perhaps a little too long in the *U* of his crotch.

"Lisa," hissed Sayla. She picked up a baby carrot and threw it into the section of her Tupperware designed for celery.

"What's wrong?" asked Leopold.

"Sayla's just being jealous," said Lisa, pausing and looking up, one hand planted between Leopold's legs.

"I am not," said Sayla. "I'm being cautious. I'm trying to prevent contaminant touch."

"Sure, Sayla," said Lisa. She finished the crotch swoop and dragged her Sharpie around Leopold's shod and lolling foot. Sayla pouted. Lisa paid no heed.

February

Lisa suggested that we attend the Sweetheart Dance.

"It's happening in the cafeteria," she said. "That's one of Manny's most-frequented locations. This is our chance to finally find the weak spot we've been searching for."

The Key Club had transformed the cafeteria. Taylor Swift bounced off the acoustic ceiling tiles while paper hearts endured a double penetration—pricked with thumbtacks, pierced with arrows. Driblets of crepe paper fluttered on the walls. Chaperones milled around the perimeter of the dance floor, making nervous jokes about teenage hormones. "That's amore!" cried a PTA mom each time she snapped a photo of a couple feigning happiness beneath an arch of pink balloons.

"There's Mr. Devine," said Lisa brightly, and she marched us over before we could protest. Mr. Devine was wearing a crumpled dress shirt and standing by the refreshment table. The Key Club had appointed him to guard the punch bowl, but instead, he was messaging Oksana.

"Hi, Mr. Devine," said Lisa in a lull between pings.

Mr. Devine looked up. "Hi, Lisa." He paused. "Hey, why are you wearing those funny plastic suits?"

"It's the style now," said Sayla, because although Mr. Devine unlocked the woodshop door for us, none of us trusted him but Lisa.

"But all the other kids are wearing normal stuff."

"We saw it in a music video," piped up Leopold.

Mr. Devine's phone pinged again. "Okay," he said. "Have fun."

We were lucky, really. One way or another, they all had their Oksanas: CrossFit, crocheting, quarterly taxes, garbage and recycling on different days, ailing parents, aromatherapy, paying rent, sailboats, migraines, opioids, book clubs, hysterectomies, college football, younger women.

Mr. Devine was oblivious to our mission, but also, therefore, to the danger of the substances. The punch bowl beckoned. We'd always heard that students snuck substances into school dances, so we regarded with suspicion anyone who came too near. Could the school have assumed control of that pothead burnout wearing a bow-tie designed to look like a crumpled hundred-dollar bill? He ladled lackadaisically into a Solo cup, perhaps in an attempt to lull us before he spiked the punch with a flask of bile. Sayla growled at him. He scurried off.

Sayla protected the punch bowl. Diego took notes on the clipboard. Lisa looked at Leopold. Leopold looked at Lisa.

"Leopold," said Lisa, "would you like to dance?"

"Okay," said Leopold, but then we turned toward that seething swamp of bodies, where girls in glittery dresses ground rhythmically against their dates.

"That isn't a dance floor," said Sayla. "It's a pit of filth."

"Sayla's right," said Diego. "Let's keep our distance."

Lisa glanced around the room like a lost dog looking for its owner. We thought she might ask someone else to dance, but the other students laughed and fidgeted, and the boy in the bowtie pointed at Sayla in her plastic suit.

"I think she growled at me," we heard him say.

"What a buzzkill," said another girl and turned away.

March

Sayla insisted that the emissions stemmed from some past act of evil on the property. She researched at the library, though all she discovered was that the stenography school had produced scads of well-trained stenographers who recorded court proceedings with astounding speed.

"Not even one deadly fire or a serial-killer stenographer," said Sayla sadly. We were passing around a book related to the history of the school when Lisa flipped to a page whose margins were covered in rust-colored squiggles.

"I think it's trying to communicate!" cried Leopold. He leaned so close to the page that we worried his safety goggles might not be enough to protect the vulnerable mucus membrane of his eyes.

"I can't make it out," said Diego, squinting.

"Can anyone read shorthand?" Sayla asked. No one could.

"Maybe it means well," said Lisa. She reached out and traced her finger above the squiggles. She barely held her hand back, as if at any moment she might flick her wrist and touch the thing itself. "Maybe the school is just like us, but, like, a bigger body and the substances it emits are like the substances we emit, because—let's be real—all of us poop and pee and throw up and sweat and vomit and wipe our runny noses, and it's no big deal."

"I have to return this book tomorrow or I'll be fined," said Sayla after a moment of stupefied silence. She closed the book and stuck it in her backpack. The spell broke. Lisa immersed her errant hand in a snack-sized bag of SunChips.

"I saw leftover diarrhea water in the boy's third-floor bathroom," said Leopold.

"Sighting time and detailed description?" asked Diego as he took down the clipboard from the wall.

April

Every Easter Lisa's family drove to Idaho to visit her grandparents and she missed an extra day of school. During her absence, we met at the landing and tallied her transgressions.

First, although it had never previously occurred to us, we began to mistrust her skill with watercolor. Paint, after all, was just another substance. We found it suspicious that her paint did exactly what she wanted, while our paint blossomed strangely and soaked into the cheap thin paper that the school provided.

She had so many freckles on her body—they formed freckled chains that were almost, one might say, like a series of rust-colored squiggles communicating some kind of sacrilegious shorthand message. And, frankly, she was just too friendly. Although we valued the landing, we began to suspect that Mr. Devine unlocked the door for Lisa because he secretly desired to make substances with her. We suspected Leopold of the same offense.

"No," Leopold insisted. He was eating reduced-sodium salami stacked between two slices of white bread. "I don't care about Lisa. She freaks me out."

"She admits her own emissions," said Diego.

"She *revels* in them," said Leopold. "She's as eager as Manny."

"She can't even keep her words clean," added Sayla. "She's always using nonstandard contractions like *m'kay* and *must've* and *c'mon*."

"We should correct her," said Leopold.

"We should kill her," said Sayla.

"We should pass a series of new injunctions that will force her from the group," said Diego.

We settled on Diego's idea, because killing seemed certain to produce more substances.

On the Monday after Easter, we posted a bulletin on the woodshop door that announced the prohibition of all nonstandard contractions, the possession of more than twenty-five freckles, non-novice watercolor skills, maintaining friendly relationships outside of the group, and human-to-human substance creation, which, of course, had always been forbidden, but never in a formal way.

May

Lisa hadn't shown up for the past four days—we congratulated ourselves on her successful expulsion. During our period of anti-Lisa legislation, we had tabled all other initiatives. Now we debated the formal censure of open-toed shoes. Sayla skipped ahead as we climbed the stairs to the landing. Leopold sealed us inside.

Then we heard footsteps crunching slowly up the metal stairs. We knew it was Lisa. We could feel her germy hands as they dragged across the railing, her dirty shoes as they smeared the sterile, sacred stairs.

"You're not welcome here!" cried Sayla, but Lisa kept on climbing. Step by step, her body built itself as she ascended. She was still wearing her protective suit, but she had ripped it open down the front and we could see her street clothes peeking out from underneath.

"Hi, friends," she said, and her words felt like salt on a wound, a raw pink ooze that made us cower. "Long time no see."

She took her spot beside Diego, and we all gazed crazily around the circle, avoiding Lisa's eyes. She held a tray from the cafeteria that she'd heaped with taboos: a spork speared through a slab of Mexican lasagna, a carton of milk, a gob of sour cream.

"Student #1097," said Diego finally. It was her student code. We only called each other by our names. "You are in violation of a series of recent injunctions and must leave the woodshop space immediately."

"Mmmmm, no thanks," said Lisa, and then she did a truly heinous thing. She reached behind her, grabbed a jar from the sealed collection of samples, and unscrewed the lid. We felt the spores drift up and overtake the landing.

"Retreat!" cried Diego, and we all leapt up and clattered down the stairs.

"Is everything okay back there?" called Mr. Devine.

"We're fine," Diego yelled. "We're celebrating. Sayla just got her scores back on a calc test." When we heard the clack of Mr. Devine's keyboard a moment later, we breathed a sigh of relief.

In the woodshop proper, we regrouped. Diego reached beneath a workbench and removed our emergency cache: squirt guns and a Costco-sized tub of sanitizer. We loaded the guns and then distributed them among ourselves. A moment later, Sayla ripped off her gloves and shot her gun into her hands.

"Goddammit, Sayla," said Leopold as we watched Sayla's chapped red skin absorb our ammunition. Sayla kept rubbing and rubbing and rubbing. She reminded us of that scene in Shakespeare that we strongly disliked— the one where Lady Macbeth faces a substance so insidious that she can't get it off of her hands.

"Are you contaminated?" demanded Leopold. "Do we need to establish a quarantine zone?"

"Hold up!" cried Diego. "Sayla, pull yourself together. Leopold, don't you see? The substances are trying to divide us. We have to go in as a seamless unit. One mind, one body. Secure in our purity no matter what we see."

He looked around the circle. "Are we ready?"

"Ready," we said. We squared our shoulders. We raised our guns. For the second time that day, we climbed the stairs.

She was kneeling in the center of the landing with all of the sample jars spread open at her feet. She licked her finger as we watched, swirled it around one of the jars, then licked her finger again. A brown substance smudged the edges of her mouth.

"Lisa, no," begged Leopold, and for a moment, we thought that she might listen. It was Leopold who had invited her to join our group. It was Leopold whom she had always loved.

"Hungry?" she asked, and she dumped the gray-green contents of another jar across her tray of food and took up a heaping sporkful of lasagna. We stood there paralyzed: horrified, fascinated, incredulous, aroused, unbelieving.

"O Omnipotent Unpolluted One, protect us," whispered Diego. Then he raised his gun and fired. The shot hit Lisa on the forehead, but it did not seem to burn. She massaged the sanitizer into her face.

"Piss off," she said.

At that moment, Sayla turned and fled, and the rest of us followed, leaving Mr. Devine and his distant lover alone in the woodshop with the newly formed avatar of filth.

June

We relocated to an abandoned supply closet on the second floor. We taught ourselves shorthand, waited for another book to speak.

We observed how Manny greeted Lisa. "Have a good day," he would say. "Thanks for all you do," she would answer.

At first we carried out patrols, but although the substances continued to appear, Lisa didn't seem to notice. Sometimes we passed her laughing in the halls, but she didn't flinch or back away or declare her allegiance to the substances. We had known her since elementary school, but now it felt like we, who were all the world, had shrunk to nothing. She avoided our eyes like the others. She never spoke to us again.

We didn't want to speak to her, of course, but it bothered us to never get an answer. Had we hurt her so badly that she attempted suicide by eating substances? Was she finally giving in to the urge that we had first noticed when she nearly touched the rust-colored squiggles? Had the substances seduced her, or had she always been their spy? We wondered if she experienced agony or ecstasy when the poop-paprika sizzled on her tongue. We wondered what she did with her life now that we were not a part of it.

On the last day of school, we stood at the entrance waiting for our parents to pick us up.

We would spend the next three months in the haphazard pollution of our homes, where our mothers dragged damp rags over dusty bureaus and a pink film filled the grout between the shower tiles. There was no order there, no malevolent organism orchestrating the discharge of the substances. Things were sometimes dirty, that was all.

"We'll meet every Wednesday to build our strategy for senior year," said Diego.

"I believe we need to adopt a more aggressive approach," said Sayla.

"Look," interrupted Leopold. "There's Lisa."

She was wearing a spaghetti strap tank top. Freckles shone on her arms and back, rose up from between her breasts, and dappled her face. Her hair, unnetted, bounced on her shoulders.

She wasn't wearing a bra. Her breasts bounced too. She ran down the front steps, crossing above the school motto etched into the riser: "Provehito in Altum"—"Launch Forth into the Deep." It was sunny outside. We could see her shadow as it broke across the stairs, the black smear of her body on the gray cement. She looked up once and met our eyes and then she crossed the street and turned the corner. Her body vanished. We could still see the pattern of her freckles. They hung like motes before our eyes.

Mothers

I wanted to picture how big my baby was, so I typed in "how big" and the autofill popped up before I could finish. Did I want to know the size of bedbugs, wind turbines, dorm rooms, dust mites, Dobermans, mitochondria, or Minecraft worlds? I did not. A website called Fetal Fruits promised me a week-by-week comparison, though several times the slideshow replaced fruit with the image of a suitably-sized vegetable—I learned that at thirty weeks my baby would reach the length of a bunch of leeks. The final slide was a photo of a newborn. "Congratulations!" the caption read. "Your baby is no longer a piece of fruit."

But she was none of these things: neither a leek nor a living baby. She was twenty weeks. She was the size of a large mango, not a small one—the green mangos with the red blush, not the yellow mangos that I could cover with one hand. Mango, I thought, getting excited. Baby Mango. My Mangosteen Tree. Mangosteen is a different kind of fruit, much smaller than my baby, but I still liked the sound of the name.

My mother used to call me her dearest dearbug, but one day voice-to-text garbled the message and I became her dearest yearbook. Ever after, when I imagined myself in relation to her, I imagined high school yearbooks stacked on a podium and me standing on the tallest tier—the winner, the one thing she would carry from the burning house. Isn't that the question you're supposed to ask when you really want to know a stranger? The boring ones say their passports or their computers or their wedding rings. The vain ones want the framed erotic photo of themselves that they hung above their beds. But the good mothers understand that they are being asked to name what they love most. "I would carry my daughter," they answer. "She is the dearest yearbook I own, the most beloved bug, the sweetest mango, I would carry my daughter out of the house."

Last week I went into the city. It was October, a crisp blue day, and leaves scooted over sidewalks in the wind.

The closer I got, the rougher the road; asphalt blighted six ways from Sunday, and me trying to miss potholes and somehow running them down. Carrie was away on a work trip. She didn't have to know unless I brought the car back with a bent rim or some kind of weird vibration, and then there would be hell to pay, but still I drove.

My mom lives in an old brick bungalow between a burndown and an urban farm. It was the home where she grew up, where I was born, where she will die. She gave birth to me in a big plastic trough that my father bought for that very purpose. They wanted to protect their mattress from the blood. They wanted to protect me from the hospital. Carrie assures me that things are better now, but I don't know. Carrie was born in a hospital.

Squash grew in the garden next door. As I walked up the drive, I could see the fetus delicata, larger than my baby, rubbing their tough yellow curves in the dirt. On the other side of my mother's property, the burndown tried to pass itself off as an ordinary house. Fire had blacked the brick around the doors and windows, but the exterior was otherwise untouched. I could almost believe that the Arreolas were eating chilaquiles in the kitchen, except that the windows had shattered and the doors had incinerated and I could see straight through to the other side, where the backyard, wild and verdant, had forced its way past the half-fallen fence.

"My dearest yearbook," said my mother when she opened the door. She was wearing a ripped sweater, mustard-colored, so old it seemed to have shifted its materiality and become a piece of chamois, soft and worn. She hugged me seamlessly, as if my belly hardly mattered. After a few moments, I pulled myself away and went inside to use the bathroom. Baby Mango had been pressing on my bladder for the past five miles, but I hadn't stopped at any of the corner stores. They were the kind of stores with Snapple on sale for 79 cents and banners promising "Bread – Milk – Beer – Tobacco." I didn't like that feeling anymore, rows of cigarettes behind the register and the store clerk staring at my belly like he could pierce through all my layers of protection—coat, shirt, skin, muscle—and rake his eyes across my sacred Mango.

It was cold inside my mother's house. She always stinted on the heat, even though she knew that Carrie and I would help her with the bills. Sometimes, if my Uncle Mark delivered a cord of wood from his farm up north, she wouldn't even bother to turn the boiler on. I wondered if it changed the quality of her dreams, those early morning hours when the fire was dying in the grate and she breathed on the couch beneath five woolen blankets. I wondered if she dreamed about black dogs weighing down her chest, about lying underwater with her arms crossed, about a deep and smothering embrace.

She was sitting in her recliner when I came back to the living room. I pulled up a chair and sat across from her. I could hear the click of the radiator—she'd upped the heat while I was in the bathroom. We'd texted a few times about the pregnancy, but she hadn't seen me in the past five months and her eyes kept drifting towards my belly. She was skating a pair of tweezers over her chin, feeling with the tips of her fingers for the coarse dark hairs. She inspected each hair as she plucked it out, judging how deeply it had rooted in her skin.

"How've you been, Mom?"

"Fine, except that hippie farmer next door is bringing all his hippie friends to stay."

"Aw, c'mon, Mom. You're not exactly mainstream. What do you care if some young person wants to live a quote-unquote alternative lifestyle?"

"They make a racket all night long and I can't sleep."

"He's an Inoc?"

"Of course he is," she snapped. "An organic farmer, too. Wants to avoid all of the toxins and pesticides because his parents injected him in utero. Whenever I see him he asks about my dreams. His name is Thom—Thom with an h, but I think the spelling is an affectation."

"I bet his parents actually named him Thom."

"What kind of parents would do that to a child?"

"Like you have the right to criticize."

"I named you Roya for a reason."

"Carrie's friends sure get a kick out of it."

Carrie's name hung coolly in the air between us. I broke my mother's gaze and glanced around the living room. Ever since my dad died, her knickknacks had run rampant—ceramic roosters, slender angels, and, because of Halloween, a whole collection of finger puppet monsters with thin plastic arms that waved on the shelf when I moved.

"I guess if you're here then Carrie must be on a work trip."

"She's in New Orleans. She's getting back tonight."

"And the baby's doing fine?"

"Uh-huh. Everything normal. A girl—I think I told you that. We have a check-up appointment tomorrow."

"Twenty weeks. That's an important developmental milestone."

"Sure, Mom."

"You're due in February?"

"Valentine's Day."

She grimaced, plucked another hair.

"Due dates are just estimates."

"Carrie and I would like that, though."

"Just don't name your baby Lovella or something dumb like that."

Carrie and I were considering Rose or Ruby to fit with the Valentine's theme, but I didn't think my mother had the right to criticize. Forty years ago, after the discovery of an inoculation that eliminated the biological need for sleep, so-called protest names came into style. I was born a decade later, on the tail end of the resistance movement, but my mother still named me Roya, the Persian word for "dreams." Now there were no new Royas, just a bunch of thirty- and forty-somethings who had to field awkward questions when baristas scrawled our names onto our coffee cups. "Do you still sleep?" the gape-mouthed Inocs asked, followed, inevitably, by that unanswerable question—"What is it like to dream?"—as if they expected that I could describe an entire world in the time it took to make a macchiato. But it was not so much a question as an emanation of longing. They knew that they had lost the ability to comprehend.

"You're getting enough rest?" my mother asked.

"Sure, most of the time. I have to sleep on my side now because of the baby and it drives me crazy, but of course Carrie doesn't understand. She thinks sleep's just a matter of closing my eyes."

"And Carrie doesn't pressure you to inoculate the baby?"

"Carrie supports me, Mom."

"I'm not just talking about money, sweetheart."

"I'm not either. We're making the choice together."

She tapped her tweezers across her chin as if she were searching for a soft spot, like the bitter rot on the bottom of an apple.

"So where're you having the baby?"

"St. Luke's."

"Be careful, Roya," said my mother. "They used to steal newborns at the hospitals and inoculate them against the mother's will."

"Now everyone inoculates," I pointed out. "Stealing is unnecessary."

"Not everyone." She dragged a hair from her chin. It was as long and dark as an eyelash. Make a wish, I almost said. I thought of the plastic trough, me coming into being in the kitchen. That was thirty years ago, back when the house next door had an interior, back when the sodium lights turned on at eight o'clock. When I was born my mother decided to refuse the world, and then she decided to never take it back. She thought I was a vassal, not a lover; a patsy, not a partner; an easy mark, not a careful mother. She couldn't understand that I would make a different wish.

I spent another hour at my mom's house. Our conversation never made it past that edge. Afterwards, she narrated in detail the plot of a show I didn't watch and gave me a finger puppet that I stuffed into the glove box. I knew I would forget about it and that one day it would pop out when Carrie asked me to grab something. I imagined Carrie saying, with a cute little sneer, "What is *that*?"

I didn't go home. I drove to the Detroit Institute of Arts, ten minutes from my mother's house. It was Wednesday, 1 p.m., totally empty. The woman at the coat check was wearing a name tag with my name. She was my age, with a long, glossy sheet of black hair. Another Roya, taking coats and giving tokens. All those righteous and resistant mothers, christening their daughters with righteous and resistant names.

"I'm Roya, too," I murmured as I leaned over the counter and handed her my coat. It was a coat Carrie liked, soft and maroon, with a shearling collar that I clutched around my neck on windy days.

"Last night I dreamed that an alien was playing the piano and whenever I got too close he would turn yellow and glow," she said.

"Last night I dreamed that I was in Maui with my wife and Maui had a bear problem and a bear jumped into our pool, but instead of a bear, it was a person," I answered. It was traditional among Nonocs— non-inoculated people—to greet each other with the telling of our dreams.

"I'm glad to meet you," she said, except she wasn't looking at me. She was gazing at my belly. She had hungry eyes.

"What will you name your baby?" she asked.

"Rose or Ruby, we think."

"Not another Roya?"

"No, we've decided not to pass that on."

She looked up from my belly and into my eyes.

"I understand," she said, dropping a coat check token into my hand. It was a coin, so cold it felt like water. I stuck it in my pocket and then she nodded, cool and polite, and turned back to the sliver of the world over which she held dominion.

There was a place I always went to in the Institute, ever since I was a little girl. It was in the photography section, a photo by John Dugdale called "The Turbulent Dream." Sepia. Smaller than a sheet of printer paper. The photo showed a naked woman sitting in a kitchen. She had short hair like mine and a chain around her neck, and she was resting her head on a table. Not cheek down like a tired child but mashing her face against the wood. There was a vase full of flowers by her head, dogwoods, perhaps—they were frowsy and wilted, spilling petals everywhere like salt. They spilled onto the table and across her head, following her hair where it arrowed neatly on the back of her neck. Because her face was hidden, I could not tell if her eyes were open or closed, if she were smiling or weeping, dreaming or waiting, resting or cursing the world.

I didn't deny the importance of the waking world. Ten years before my birth, at the advent of inoculation, our leaders proclaimed that we could only save ourselves by ending sleep. People resisted at first. Mothers marched on hospitals and "dream on" graffiti covered the city, but no one could come up with a clear defense of dreams. Perhaps dreams allowed us to express unconscious desires or process information or practice emotional moments in a safe state, or perhaps they were merely a meaningless symptom of sleep. Slowly, slowly, we turned against our dreams. How could we cure cancer, climate change, poverty, partisanship, if first we didn't cure sleep? Our bodies demanded that we spend eight hours doing nothing every night, even as the world unwound around our beds.

And now the world had stopped unwinding and I had not contributed. I accepted my uselessness as I gazed at the woman in the photo. As a minor, I could have petitioned for court-ordered inoculation; at eighteen, I could have walked into any hospital at any time. Although inoculation worked best when delivered in utero, I could have cut my sleep time down to three or four hours every night. Still, I refused. It wasn't because I had some cogent defense of dreams. Sometimes when Carrie pressed me I would throw up my hands. I only knew that I was thirty, I had spent a third of my life dreaming. Ten years was a world unto itself. I was glad that they had saved this one, this waking world, but I was glad that I had saved that other one, too.

I did not stop at the coat check when I left the museum. I hoped Roya would have the chance to take the shearling coat that Carrie loved, to brush her hand to her throat as she clutched the collar close. Her back was turned when I walked past. I felt relief. I tossed my coat check token into the fountain and drove back to the suburbs—I wanted to have time to neaten the house before I picked up Carrie from the airport. The car made a tink tink tink sound as it cooled in the garage, as pristine as it had been before the city.

I used to have a friend, another dreaming woman whose mother refused inoculation. She couldn't find a job, so she performed magic tricks at Eastern Market. She called each of her tricks a dream. Watch my dreams, she would say to passersby. They could never resist—they watched with horror, fascination, longing, greed. One of the dreams she shared was a knot trick. The knot looked sturdy, but then it slipped apart. She taught them this—that in dreams the most secure knot can unravel. The knot she used was called a grief knot. When I heard the name, I was sure it held a deeper meaning. No, she said, laughing. Each of her front teeth had a brown stain. She explained that the knot combines the features of a reef knot, a thief knot, and a granny knot. It's a portmanteau, not a metaphor. Grief has no meaning, she said.

I was lying on my side when Carrie nestled next to me, pressing her face close to mine. She licked my nose and I squealed. She kissed my lips and I sighed.

"Miss me?" Carrie asked. The inside of her lips had turned purple from the wine she'd had with dinner. She was still wearing her travelling clothes, including a silk scarf that I disliked. She must have worn it to protect herself from the chill of the airplane, but it was too flouncy—it reminded me of something from my mother's house. I unknotted it from around her neck.

"You should rest," I said. "Take a bath or something."

I knew she would spend the rest of the night in the study, catching up. That was her role in our relationship. Inocs took more classes. Held more degrees. Worked longer hours. Nonocs found it nearly impossible to find high-level jobs. We were janitors, dishwashers, buskers, the takers of coats. We went to school on special scholarships and enrolled for a quarter-load of classes. We met beautiful women getting law degrees and surrendered ourselves. Housewives. Homeless. Brown stains on our front teeth or perfect smiles from our wives' insurance. Inocs married Nonocs all the time. Honestly, I think we kept them sane. Our spouses didn't have to see us 24-7—many a marriage saved by one of its members going to bed. We cleaned their houses, cooked their meals, carried their babies. We had the time to be domestic. They had the time to work hundred-hour weeks.

"You are the rester," said Carrie. "And I am the worker bee."

I rolled my eyes

"Well, I am growing our child. It does require some effort."

"Oh, stop. You know I know that."

"I know."

She nuzzled me.

"Tell me about our baby."

"She's the size of a mango now."

Carrie purred.

"I thought we could call her Mango Baby."

"Oh," said Carrie, widening her eyes with mock disappointment. "But I liked Peanut."

"Kumquat," I corrected, one of the Fetal Fruits that I remembered from the slideshow. "But that was weeks ago. She's growing. I'm growing."

She placed her hands on my belly. She always made me feel as if I were just right. I thought of driving into the

city, my cold mother curled in her recliner, her angel gew-
gaws gazing down their noses at her dreams.

"I visited my mom today," I blurted.

Carrie leaned back, carrying her purple lips away
from mine.

"How'd she seem? I hope she didn't upset you."

"Fine. Annoyed at her neighbors, like that's new. She
can't bear to ask if we're going to inoculate, so instead
she's spinning stories. She keeps warning me that they'll
steal the baby at the hospital and do it then—that's what
she'll tell herself when she meets her granddaughter who
never sleeps."

"She's living in a dream world, Roya. Apropos, I
guess." She brushed her lips against my forehead. "I love
you and I chose you. When I take a break from work
and peek into the bedroom and I see you sleeping and
I see your belly, I never doubt my choice. I don't want to
change you, I'm just asking that you take a step back and
consider. We can give our baby a small world with dreams
or a big world without them, and I am saying—let's give
our daughter the bigger world."

I didn't have anything to say, and so I lay there silently
in Carrie's arms. She rocked me gently and the baby
rocked inside of me, asleep but not dreaming. Dreams
came later, at twenty-three weeks. A few minutes passed
and I found myself in that space between waking and

sleeping where my thoughts warped into strange forms that still felt reasonable. It was a state of being that Carrie didn't even know existed, that our baby would never know existed, and I wrenched my eyes open and castigated my brain for accepting insanity so easily. I wanted to think longer about the world that we were giving to our baby, so I tried to stay awake. Instead I zipped a horse into a violin case and found nothing amiss in the act.

When we introduce ourselves, Carrie's friends always compliment my name. There was a huge boom in Royas forty years ago, but now it's perceived as exotic. Sometimes Carrie pretends that her friends meant to compliment her. "Oh thank you," she says, batting her eyes. "I love my name." I always thought it was a joke, a way of avoiding predictable questions, but once in bed she confessed her secret earnestness. She heard herself inside of every conversation. The very commonness that people did not compliment was the very quality that made her sing.

Shoppers carry groceries. Trains carry passengers. Stories carry meaning—perhaps the same is true of dreams. My mother can carry a tune. My father never could. People would drop whatever they were carrying and stop their ears. That trait has carried over into me.

I am carrying a child. Carrie carries a briefcase. When I met her, I liked how she carried herself, upright and unyielding, as if she possessed a silver spine.

"I carried you out of poverty," said Carrie. "And I carried you into my life."

Our appointment was at nine the next morning. The P.A. called our name and led us down the corridor to the ultrasound room. It was airless, unabashedly beige. The walls were bare. I propped myself up on the examination table and Carrie grabbed a chair. She was wearing that scarf again, the one I did not like.

"So I see this is a bit of an unusual situation," said Dr. Singh, paging through her notes. "It seems that you, Roya, are a non-inoculated person."

"That's correct," I said. I didn't think Dr. Singh could discern it, but I could hear the quiver in my voice, like a plastic comb running over a piece of cellophane. "My parents were objectors."

"And you understand that while the inoculation is not as effective when administered to adults, it can still be given?"

"I understand that I could still receive it, yes."

"Actually," interjected Carrie, "what my wife *really* understands is her constitutional right to refuse. And not to be coerced, I might add." She always turned a little pink when she defended me.

"Of course," said Dr. Singh. "I only want to make sure that she is aware of her options. As the carrying mother, it is also her right to refuse to inoculate the fetus, at which point the noncarrying parent can submit a petition to the court."

"No, I want to move ahead," I said. "I want to inoculate my baby."

Dr. Singh smiled, curt but real.

"I think you're making a very wise choice. Best to nip it in the bud."

I signed my name to a clipboard's worth of paperwork and the P.A. applied a transdermal patch to my belly, some kind of tranquilizer to keep the baby calm. Then she tucked a sterile drape around the ultrasound site and scooped orange goop onto my stomach. I shivered when the transducer touched my skin. I was staring at the ceiling. It was the only part of the room with any decoration. They had patterned the pages from a calendar up there—garish sunsets, red and gold. I turned my head to see the screen. There was our baby on the ultrasound, grainy and lumpy, with a giant head.

Dr. Singh left the room and returned with the uterine syringe. She removed the safety cap. It was a four-inch needle, so thin it looked like a stiffened piece of silver thread. Carrie squeezed my hand.

"Are you ready?" asked Dr. Singh.

"I am."

"This is the needle," said Dr. Singh. "Keep your elbows by your side. This is the insertion—"

It felt like the pinch of two hot fingers. The needle appeared on the screen as a slash of light. It looked like a comet streaking towards my baby.

"One moment," said Dr. Singh. I felt my belly cramp when the needle entered my uterus. The tip dipped towards the baby. Resist or receive, I didn't care how she reacted, I only wanted her to show her choice. If she flinched, I would have thrown myself from the exam table. If she moved towards the needle, I would have kissed Carrie's hand.

"This is the injection—" Dr. Singh depressed the plunger. The inoculation uncoiled inside of me. The needle retracted. The baby remained. My Baby Mango, dreamless as a piece of fruit forevermore. I thought of everything that she could be—a janitor, a dishwasher, a busker, a taker of coats, but also a ballerina, a broker, an actuary, an artist, an engineer. I didn't care what she was, whether she became the most successful biochemist in Michigan or simply made ends meet with some dumb job. I only wanted every-thing for her because she was everything to me. I wanted the high and the low. I wanted the world laid out inside her body, and to do that, I had to take away her dreams.

"It's okay to cry," said Carrie. "I know it's bittersweet."
I realized that I was crushing Carrie's hand. I let her go,
then caught her up again and laced her fingers into mine.
I thought of the knot as it slid into nothing. Reef, thief,
granny, grief. I didn't care what my friend said—I knew
that there was meaning in the name.

I went to bed early that night, hoping to dream something significant. It was a dumb wish—the kind of thing
an Inoc would imagine, that dreamers can summon certain dreams. Many years ago, when my father died, I des-
perately wanted to see him again. I pictured his face every
night before I fell asleep. Every night I dreamed a new
inanity. I never understood where my dreams came from,
why they happened, what they meant. They poured out
from between my fingers like solid rock becoming sand.
They unraveled into separateness inside my hands.

Months passed. I recorded my dreams in a journal. I
put a child in a box and left her there while I sang kara-
oke. I saw my mother who was not my mother, but a thin
old man. I swallowed a fly that had fallen in a glass of
water and gave birth to a human baby with skin that glis-
tened like an insect's wing. I reached into my mouth and
removed a tooth as large as a cauldron. A cake smiled
and danced in the air and when I touched it, it became a

crown. I pulled hard-boiled eggs from a bucket and with each new egg another branch erupted from my head. I drove off a bridge and awoke instead of dying. I tended a plant that consumed me, and even when I knew it would, I gave it more.

Then one night I dreamed that the police had surrounded me in a basement and I faced a stone wall with a gate at its center. I had nowhere to go—I thrust myself through the gate and fell into the mountains. I was descending on a narrow, rocky path. All of a sudden I became aware of a presence. I looked to my right, then to my left, and I saw bears walking on either side of me. I sensed that if I took one wrong step they would break from their paths and rip me apart. I was scared. My heart pounded. I walked with my eyes straight ahead and then, farther down the path, I saw another person. It was my father. I hurried to overtake him, but I did not run. I walked beside him and the bears walked beside us, but everything had changed—everything had become all right. "Is it you?" I asked. "Yes," he answered, and he took my hand.

My father had his father's name, which was also the name of his father's father. Such silly men, pouring themselves into their patronyms. I knew that what was good in my baby was not the same as what was good in me. Didn't every mother have to realize that? I was Roya, she was not. When I woke that night, I could feel the edge of my dream curling away like a piece of burning paper. I spoke to my belly, but I did not sing. I whispered, though there was no one it was possible to wake.

"Rosie," I said, with my hands on my belly, and I began to tell her what I dreamed.

Double or Nothing

On our first date he pretended to be Orson Welles in *The Third Man* as we sat in the Ferris wheel gazing out across the bay. He delivered the lines with the pleasure of a ham, waving his arms so that the pod swung back and forth. I felt an extra thrill of terror. Something about that feeling of suspension, hanging above the unimaginable vastness of the water and the unimaginable profusion of the people, made me remember that moment long after all the other details of my first and lonely life had faded back to sepia.

"Tell me," he cried, eyes bulging, "if I had the power to touch a dot down there and simply wipe it out, would you really feel any pity? Would you really try to stop me?"

"It's a weird line for a first date," I said. I had swiped right on Tinder because I liked the oddness of his profile pic—two snarling cats with identical markings, one in each of his gloved hands.

"It's the only Ferris wheel scene I know."

"*Never Been Kissed*," I countered. I had a thing for Drew Barrymore—her broad cheeks and her blunt nose, like she'd been cast in wax from an inexact but beautiful mold. I liked her wild child persona, flashing David Letterman as she danced atop his desk, and the fact that under it all you could tell that she was scared and confused, a wound more than a person, and that that wound, which seemed irreparable, had somehow healed with age.

"I've never seen it."

"A journalist goes undercover as a high school student and falls in love with her English teacher. They ride the Ferris wheel together."

"Sounds kinda creepy."

"In retrospect, yeah."

"Ever bring your students up here?"

"They're kindergarteners," I answered. "They're three-foot-something. It's a height issue—they couldn't get on. Also, like, a liability issue. But in the context of the movie, it was sweet."

"That makes sense," he said, even though nothing made sense—not the premise of the movie nor the fact that he was wearing gloves. They were the same pair I'd noticed in his profile pic, and he wore them despite the

fact that it was sixty-eight degrees and halfway sunny. Still,
I found him strangely endearing. Earlier, pondering a pipe-
fish at the aquarium, he'd bent down and gazed with the
same intensity that he later paid to the showier exhibits. He
seemed to make no distinction between the ordinary and
extraordinary—as if being mottled and gray were the same
as being mottled and yellow or fringed and speckled with
gold. I liked that. His face announced at every moment that
it was worth looking closely at the world.

We'd been paused at the top, but now the wheel turned
again and our pod left the hordes on the boardwalk and
glided out above the dirty water of the bay. I found myself
trapped in that trough of awkwardness that I often fell into
on first dates—those moments after I'd exhausted all the
superficial get-to-know-you's and I didn't know what to
say. It was our final revolution. The couple in the pod ahead
of us sucked face with impressive dedication, as if they'd be
parted forever when their feet returned to the earth.

"It's nice to have someone to talk to," I murmured.
"That's what Drew Barrymore says when she's on the
Ferris wheel with her English teacher. It's a better line
than homicidal Orson Welles."

"That's true," he said.

And then he shifted and our shoulders touched as
if by accident. I let my arm fall loose so that it leaned
against his. I imagined our bodies zipping together down

the seam of our sides. We tore our eyes away from the face suckers in front of us and looked down through the transparent floor at the people-dots on the promenade, the parents pushing thousand-dollar strollers and the baseball hats hiding faces and the headphones hiding ears and the scraps of summer clothing hiding nothing—so many limbs, slender, stocky, sun-kissed, light, and dark. No single person looked any bigger than my big toe. I can still see the polish on it, so vividly do I remember, a coating of pearlescent pink that sparkled with the same sheen as the water.

He always wore a pair of gray nylon gloves with a fold-back tip on the index finger that he never folded back. We'd been sleeping together since the second week and I had seen the rest of him, especially the bareness of his back as he got out of bed to use the bathroom. Still, I had never seen his hands. He caressed me with the gloves; he slept beside me, gloved; and when he clasped me after showering, the gloves were wet.

"Can you tell me?" I would ask. I assumed some unspeakable disfigurement. When he swapped his wet gloves for a dry pair, he changed in the corner with his back to me. His studio had the blandness I had come to expect from the men I met on Tinder: a bed, a desk-cum-kitchen-table, a bureau that seemed to have the power to draw clothes close, but not contain them— he kept his clothes in a laundry basket that brushed the bureau's side. Gloves were the only evidence of plenitude. They spilled out from his closet when I opened the door.

"I find it difficult to talk about," he would answer, wearing such a hangdog look that he put me off from asking till another interval of tenderness had passed. In the beginning, our attachment seemed to double every week. I referred to this doubling as an interval of tenderness, though later I learned that it was not a stable measure— that the longer we knew each other, the longer it took for our closeness to double again. But when we started dating, that newness swept me up. I loved to stretch out next to him, propped up on my elbows as I drew hieroglyphics on his back. I could spend entire mornings that way, the lazy Sundays of our first summer. He would lie on his stomach with his face to one side and look so calm and satisfied that I felt like I could drug him with my fingertips.

During the eighth interval of tenderness, I had a habit of leaving his apartment and going straight to work. Sometimes I looked so disheveled that the children glanced at me with nervous sympathy. It was finally Sheila who spoke.

"Ms. Emily," she said. "Did your mommy stop fixing your hair?" It was Sheila who came back from Tijuana with one half of her head covered in cornrows and the other half a frizzy mess, her mother having given up midway through the process of unbraiding. Having witnessed other parents struggle with the task, I could have told her—it was best to snip the tips.

The pace of doubling had slowed by then. It took four weeks for us to know each other twice as well, though it still felt like a headlong rush. There was so much to do, so much to know, so much to touch. We'd been dating officially for four months. And it was at some point during this period, the eighth interval of tenderness, that I taught the children how to estimate.

As part of the lesson, I wove through the tables and the knee-high chairs carrying a tray of rubber bands. The construction paper letters in the window threw shadows on the floor. I stepped through a *W* and avoided a toy car that had escaped from one of the storage bins. It smelled like graham crackers and the peculiar miasma that comes from seventeen five-year-old bodies in a poorly ventilated room.

"Guess how many rubber bands," I said. I had counted out twenty-six. They lay in a pile like pink snakes. My students stayed in their seats because I told them to, but their whole bodies strained with the performance of that novel act.

"There are forty, Ms. Emily," said Sheila, who was testing at a second-grade level.

"One hundred," said Skylar, who looked like a mini-copy of my mother, fat red cheeks and hair so blonde it seemed to have no color.

"Twenty," said Aden, not because he was a gifted esti-mator, but because he didn't yet grasp the existence of a higher number.

But the boy who sat beside them, he guessed none.

"Lloyd," I said in my sweetest teacher voice. "Can't you see that there is something on the tray?"

On that night in my apartment, after ten intervals of ten-derness, he held up his hand and folded back the tip of the glove. His finger poked out like any other finger, no burns or warts or swelling or discoloration. I felt that I'd been tricked.

"Wait," he said, and he touched the cinnamon-scented candle on my coffee table. There was no pop or flash of lightning. It was all very ordinary. It was like I'd blinked my eyes without blinking and suddenly there were two candles side by side.

"Were there always two?" I asked.

"No."

"Do it again." I felt as greedy as my students.

"I can't. I can only double twice a day. Three times and I'm nearly comatose."

"You've only done it once."

"Twice," he said, folding the flap over his index finger so that another pair of gray nylon gloves appeared on my carpeted floor. He was panting slightly, leaning back into the plushness of the couch.

Later I insisted that we burn the second candle to verify that he had replicated the essence of the thing. I could no longer remember which was the original and which was the copy, so we burned them both, one after the other, while binging episodes of *Criminal Minds*. And it was true—they each smelled exactly like cinnamon.

My students made inkblot art in preparation for the Spring Open House. They took pieces of construction paper, added dabs of red, blue, and yellow paint, and then folded their papers and pressed. We talked about primary colors and secondary colors. We talked about symmetry. We unfolded their papers and pretended we were daydreaming outside.

"Imagine that you're searching for a shape in the clouds," I said. "What do you see?"

"I see a chicken in my paint," said Skylar, and one of the parent volunteers wrote "Chicken" on her paper.

"I see a rainbow rose," said Aden.

"An artichoke," said Sheila, who always had such sophisticated tastes.

"A car."

"A boot."

"I see brown," said Lloyd.

He had mashed his paper after adding too much paint. I pondered what I saw: "the holding pond for a waste treatment facility" or "the ground beneath a leaky sewer line" or "a dog turd after a deluge."

"Wow, Lloyd," I said. "That is a very original inkblot."

My boyfriend's parents called him Midas Midas, because if he touched Midas, Midas wouldn't turn gold, he would be two. He developed his powers at age thirteen, at a time when other boys were developing acne. He told me that the first thing he ever doubled was Goo, the family cat. The power struck at the same moment that he was stroking Goo's back—a feline miracle that quickly devolved into a catfight, because cats, unlike humans, cannot recognize themselves.

It was lucky, though, that the power struck at home, before he could go out and make a spectacle and get the government and the scientists involved. The first thing his parents did was glove him. Then his mother, a tax attorney with a congenital devotion to knowing every law and loophole, ran a series of experiments in the basement of their house. This was how they learned the rules.

He could only duplicate items that weighed less than two hundred pounds. Touch the page of a book and he got a second book; the petal of a flower yielded a second flower; the bead on a necklace and a whole necklace hung from his hands. His mother deduced that he never doubled partially, and that his power, therefore, could be used to identify the minimum units that made up the world. She also determined that copies contained the same imperfections as originals. Consequently, he recreated Goo with a notched ear and a crooked tail. For the rest of their lives, the two Goos hissed when they passed each other in the hall.

Only his initial touch held the power of duplication. If, say, he were to spend an hour strumming a guitar, never lifting his fingers from the strings, this act would result in a single extra copy. It was for this reason that each act of doubling ended with another pair of gloves. When he replaced the flap and the fabric touched his finger, the Law of Minimum Units decreed that he did not produce a flap, or a single glove, but an entire second pair. And although he kept his home austere—an act of protest against the reckless abundance of his body—he had an ever-replenishing supply of gloves. Every few months I would take another batch to the Salvation Army, so that the boy in charge of accepting donations took to greeting me as Madame Glove.

In the fifteen years that followed the discovery, Midas Midas had shielded his hands—only his index finger touched things without the mediation of the glove. In certain spaces he would remove the flap and revel in the joy of not creating. He hated knickknacks and loved rooms full of heavy furniture. He sought out trees, buildings, large works of public art. He adored English mastiffs, though once at the dog park he misjudged a female mastiff who turned out to be less than two hundred pounds, and we had to hustle away before the owner noticed that he now had two identical and mammoth dogs.

I drew on his back with the tip of my finger. One cat, another. The circle of the Ferris wheel going round and round and round.

"When I was a kid, I wanted everything," he said. "Two skateboards, two Slurpees, double my weekly allowance. That was my material phase, followed by my practical phase—I spent a year doubling a ten-ounce bar of gold. I wanted to be sure that me and my family would always have enough. I got sick of it, eventually—doubling felt like just another chore. And it wasn't like I could surprise myself. If you have one thing, you can imagine having two."

"You make it sound so ordinary," I said, "but it isn't ordinary to me."

And so together we discovered the third evolution of Midas Midas's power. First there was the Material Phase followed by the Practical Phase, and then, enmeshed in tenderness, the Age of Play. We had no reason for the things we did—it was simply pleasant, sometimes, to change one tube of chapstick into two, or to have two lemons in the fruit bowl with the same dimples on their peel, or two identical daffodils even though the world was full of flowers in the spring. We devoted an entire week to multiplying the spoons in my silverware drawer because I never had enough. Single socks, single earrings—but touching singletons yielded a pair, and so we ended up with three of each. He got a ring from a vending machine and doubled that, but it turned my finger green. He doubled pastries for me, a favorite pair of jeans, my car keys thrice over, and so many bras because bra shopping crushed my soul. Instead of pouring two glasses of wine, he poured one and doubled it. He filled my cupboards with wineglasses and crowded my closet with gloves. It was wasteful, I suppose, but it was also a form of welcome, a way of saying, "It is effortless to share with you."

I used instructional dominoes to teach the concept of doubling—large pieces of white cardboard that I folded down the center so that the kids could only see one side.

"Kids," I said. They were gathered on the carpet, gazing up. "If we took these three dots and doubled them, what would we have?"

"Six," said Sheila.

"Hurray," I said. I unfolded the domino and we counted together as a class.

I held up the blank domino, one half of it.

"If I doubled this," I said, "what would we have?"

"More of nothing," answered Skylar.

"Hurray," I said, unfolding the domino to prove that she was right. Lloyd stared suspiciously. He mistrusted every fundamental law.

When we returned to the Ferris wheel for our first anniversary, Midas Midas resumed his role as Orson Welles. This time, he pulled off the flap of his glove. Fourteen intervals of tenderness had passed—now it took two months for our closeness to double again.

"Tell me," he cried, pointing at the crowds, "if I had the power to touch a dot down there and simply wipe it out, would you really feel any pity? Would you really try to stop me?"

"That's not how it works," I said. Carefully, so as not to brush his finger, I reached out and gripped his elbow. He lowered his hand and replaced the flap. We sat together in silence, looking down upon the people, the additional gloves lying at our feet. I imagined we were thinking the same thing—people-dots doubling and doubling till the promenade became a work of pointillism. But I wasn't sure it would feel any different than erasing them. They seemed so small, so far away. We were all that mattered, two dots swinging high above the world.

"It's nice to have someone to talk to," I said.

"Still true," he answered, and he clasped my hand.

We dedicated our second summer to determining the minimum units that made up the world. If he touched the bun of a hamburger, he got a second hamburger. If he touched a plain bun, he got a second bun. Touching a dictionary on my bookshelf reproduced the dictionary but not the shelf, nor the daisies—tissue-paper thin—that I had pressed between the pages and forgotten. A kettle of boiling water resulted in a second kettle of boiling water, whereas room temperature water remained incidental to the kettle and was not reproduced. We'd bought our TV and remote as a set, and once, after a month of fruitless searching for the lost remote, he simply touched the TV and doubled both.

I got an IUD and we spent a month debating: Was the copper T inside my uterus incorporated within the unit of myself, or was it separate? Sometimes I imagined him touching me without the gloves. Just once—pressing his hands against my body and not letting go. He had never doubled a human, though in theory it would be no different than Goo, or the bevy of mice that he had multiplied in the basement, or the fly that blundered into his bare finger and buzzed away as two. He was willing to ponder many different doubling scenarios, including ones that I deemed cruel—doubling my Siamese fighting fish, Clancy, for example, so that we could watch Clancy fight himself. But Midas Midas shut down any talk of replicating people.

"I'm not God," he said. "And besides, it would blow my cover."

According to Midas Midas, two identical English mastiffs meant the owner had a great story for a cocktail party. But two people, two whole human beings, aware of their sameness—that was a secret that was very hard to keep.

We scoured the shore for the perfect stone. Instead we found round-bellied agates and lumps of granite veined with quartz. Midas Midas handed me a black pebble with a red band and I stuck it in my pocket. There were even golf balls sunk in the mud from some hotshot practicing his golf swing on the bluff. Finally I reached down and picked up a stone that was dull and gray and thin as a wafer. I thought that if I bit it, I could break it with my teeth.

"It's perfect," he said, and we slogged out to meet the water. We had to cross a mudflat, a vast expanse of brown that reminded me of Lloyd.

"We should take off our shoes and leave them," said Midas Midas when we'd made it halfway across. The mud had grown acquisitive. It sucked at our heels when we lifted our feet.

"We won't be able to find them on our way back," I protested. There was too much brown. We were stuck somewhere in the fifteenth interval of tenderness. Lloyd was a first-grader by then—he was Mr. Deegan's cross to bear—but when I closed my eyes, I could still picture his inkblot. The other children had been content to declare what they saw, but of course Lloyd had to hold up his paper and show me. Some of the paint had dripped down and spattered the table. Now I understood what he had made: "The way low tide bares the beach." And it was beautiful.

"Relax, Emily," said Midas Midas, a formula that always surprised him when it did not work. "If we can't find them, I'll just double you a pair."

"You can't double what isn't there," I pointed out. Eventually we settled on a landmark, one of the leftover pilings from a long-abandoned, mostly missing dock. We left our shoes beside it, laces dragging in the mud, a pair of pairs.

It smelled like sulfur, like the living soup of the bay, full of silt and fish and giant squid with eyes the size of basketballs. I knew that they were down there, deep below, living secret lives. Clouds ridged the sky like the roof of a cat's mouth. It was one of those sacred autumn days when the rain paused for long enough to confirm that the sun still existed. I could see the Olympic Mountains in the distance, impossibly tall and blue.

"Are you happy?" I asked. I loved how it felt when the mud squished up between my toes. But Midas Midas did not answer right away. He was staring at his gloves. I'd seen this mood before—sometimes, in the midst of playing with his power, he would grow morose.

"Even being out here on a beautiful day, I get sick of it," he said.

We had reached the water. The bay, smooth as glass, barely seemed to lap the shore.

"Don't worry about that right now," I said. "We have a bet to settle." Wavelets nipped at my ankles. I offered him the stone that I had found. He doubled it, then folded the flap over his finger and paused to catch his breath. A second pair of gloves floated by our feet like dead gray fish.

"Give me a second," he said. I twisted my feet back and forth to sink them deeper in the mud and pondered if the black dot bobbing in the distance was a harbor seal or a hunk of wood. Once on a sailing trip I'd heard a seal breathing off the side of the boat in the middle of the night, stertorous and yet serene. It was a memory I cherished.

"Better now?" I asked.

"Better," he said.

"Ready to cry like a baby when I kick your ass?"

"You wish."

I gripped my stone and spun it from my hand. Somehow, miraculously, it barely seemed to touch the water as it hooked across the bay. Mine skipped eight times. His skipped four. It was, I proclaimed, a natural act of doubling. None of this supernatural bullshit—I just happened to be twice as good.

"The stone," he muttered. We were heading back to the rotted piling that marked where we had stowed our shoes.

"The stone?"

"Yours must have been flatter, or something. Better for skipping."

"Nice try," I said.

"Or the gloves messed me up. I couldn't get a good grip through the gloves."

"Mmm hmm."

I reached out and stroked the back of his neck. Our shoes were sitting where we'd left them.

"See?" he said, even though I was the one who suggested that we use a landmark.

My house was full of knickknacks. I had three silver coins from Alaska, an iron hand that held a card declaring LOVE, salt and pepper shakers shaped like birds, a green Buddha, a collection of exceptional stones, and two carved wooden bears that nestled together on my coffee table. They were subtly different, which was why they fit together so well.

Sometimes, after a long day at work, I came home and noticed that the bears had moved apart. What made that happen? A mini-earthquake? A government agent tracking Midas Midas who broke into my house to search for further clues? Or Midas Midas himself, who'd touched my key to make a copy? Maybe he pushed them apart with his ungloved finger when I wasn't home. I looked in the trash to see if I could find another bear.

We attended the Picasso exhibit on a rainy afternoon in February. Sixteen intervals had passed, but I'd finally come to understand that now we halved the tenderness instead of doubling. I knew if we kept going, we would zero out.

Midas Midas stood before "The Race" and drummed his fingers on his leg. It was a painting of two women running. Their hands were clasped and raised above their heads and their shifts had fallen from their shoulders so that each woman bared a single breast. Everywhere along the walls, plaques forbade the act of touching.

"I want to touch it," he whispered, fiddling with the flap on his glove.

"Don't be silly," I hissed. I thought he was joking, but I wasn't sure. "The guards are watching. Everyone would know. And besides, we could never find a way to sell it."

"Not for the money."

"Then why?"

"Because if I doubled it, it would be less."

It was perhaps the most expensive item we had ever seen. There were, of course, the necessary acts of doubling: a diamond ring, a hundred-dollar bill, the many gold bars of his adolescence. He doubled money joylessly or not at all. But the painting piqued his interest. Two women running, four women running, eight women running—it was one of a kind. It was a riddle that Lloyd would like when he grew older: "Can doubling be the same thing as diminishment?"

"Could you double this for me?" I asked, holding out half a roll of toilet paper. "It's the last one left."

"I can't," he said. He was sitting on my couch and scrolling through his phone. "I already doubled today."

"You did?"

"A bag of chips."

"I thought we always doubled together."

"You mean you thought I always doubled when you were in the room."

"Yeah, that's what I meant."

"Because I'm the one who doubles. You watch."

"Right," I said. "And I'm the one who works. You sit at home."

"I was hungry."

"Yeah, okay."

During recess I walked the perimeter of the playground ensuring that the children did not kill each other. That was how I still kept tabs on Lloyd. He liked to occupy the center of the tire swing for the entire thirty minutes.

"It isn't fair, Ms. Emily," pouted Skylar. "He hogs the tire swing and he doesn't even use it."

Lloyd did not spin or let the black rubber touch his body, he just stood. He treated the tire swing like the portal to another world. Maybe it was. Maybe his mind was elsewhere, in a place where all the rules made sense. I imagined him learning about fractions in Mrs. Herb's

fifth grade class. If you doubled the numerator, the frac-
tion doubled. If you doubled the denominator, the frac-
tion halved. His vocabulary would have improved by then.
"Mrs. Herb," I could hear him saying, "surely you can see
this is preposterous."

I called my mom to tell her that I was planning to break
up with Midas Midas.

"I support you, honey," she said. I was drinking a beer.
I had poured the contents of the can into a wineglass,
the only type of glass I seemed to own. I fiddled with the
bears on my coffee table, pressing them together, moving
them apart.

I wanted to tell her about the time that Midas Midas
and I debated the nature of the IUD. It had been my
opinion that a copy of me would contain the copper T,
but I had also believed something more important—that
touching me would double him. Now, looking back, that
second summer struck me as the apex of our tenderness.
We had made ourselves into a minimum unit, and then
we had fallen apart.

"But who will I talk to?" I wept into the phone. "Who
will know me? How can I start again?"

"You'll be okay," she said. She was a psychologist, and
whenever she gave advice her voice took on a calming

throatiness. "You had a whole life before him. You'll have a whole life after, even though you feel so lonely now. Learn to take pleasure in yourself."

On the final interval of everything, we sat together in the Ferris wheel. He was holding a pink cloud of cotton candy anchored to a paper cone.

"Tell me," he began, "if I had the power—"

"Why do you do that?" I asked.

"I thought it cracked you up."

"I don't like it anymore."

"Okay."

"I want some cotton candy."

"Grab a piece."

"I want my own."

"I've got plenty for the two of us."

"My own," I insisted.

"Fine," he said. He pulled back the flap of his glove and like a flash of lightning, I reached out and clasped his hand.

Then there I was across from me looking at myself. I reached into my bag and pulled out the extra clothes that I had packed.

"Emily," said Midas Midas. Frantically, he tucked his finger back into the glove.

"Emily Emily," I corrected.

We had the same gap between our front teeth. We had the same green eyes, the same birthmark on our collar bones, the same IUD in our uteri that prevented other forms of reproduction. I was doubled, not diminished. We had been poised at the top of the Ferris wheel, but now we spun and spun and spun. I imagined rolling out across the bay, magically afloat. My body balanced us. We neutralized each other—it was Midas Midas who caused the pod to tilt.

"Why did you do that?" he demanded. "We could have found a way to make it work."

"No," I said. "This is the better way of ending."

"This? This is your solution? Going rogue and making a whole other human?" He was crying. I grabbed a piece of cotton candy and swabbed at the tears in his eyes. I meant it tenderly, but the sugar melted in my hands.

"It's nice to have someone to talk to," I said.

We glided to a stop. One of the operators opened the door and I informed Midas Midas that it was time for us to go. We walked in opposite directions. Me and me away from him. We lost ourselves among the people-dots. Then we heard footsteps pounding behind us and we steeled ourselves to turn around and tell him off.

"Go away," we planned to say. "We'll tell your secret if you don't leave us alone."

But it was only the operator from the Ferris wheel, breathless and red.

"Ma'am," he said.

We met his eyes.

"Ma'am," he said again, confusedly. "You left a pair of gloves behind."

Is That Sweet?

Two weeks ago, on a ledge below my windowsill, a barn swallow laid four speckled eggs no bigger than the cotton balls I use to clean my face.

"Oh Mariel, how sweet," my mother cooed over videochat. "It's a quarantine miracle."

She treats the eggs like a special dispensation—like some loving god has seen fit to send me company. But I am not impressed, because some people have partners or children or dogs, and every day, perhaps without even knowing it, they touch another living thing. Whereas I have a studio apartment without even a houseplant to my name. Now the eggs have hatched and the living things within my sphere of influence are six. There are four babies and two adults, and the adults fly away when I open the window and the babies barely seem awake. If I stretched out my hand I could reach them, but my mother reminds me not to touch.

In between bouts of copywriting, I get up and look at the babies. They lie entwined and catatonic, cupped in an orgy of contact, until their mother perches on the nest. Then they spring up, desperate to differentiate themselves. Their eyes bulge and their open mouths eclipse their bodies; their heads are too big for their thin necks and so they wobble back and forth. In two quick movements, the mother vomits into their mouths and then reaches down to swallow the soft white wad that emerges from their bare pink bottoms. Audubon Online informs me it's a fecal sac.

"Is that sweet?" I demand after detailing the process to my mother.

"Of course it is," she answers. "All care is tenderness and all tenderness is sweet." She has the camera on her laptop angled so that I can only see the bottom of her face—her yellow teeth, her jowly chin. Nothing punctures her optimism, not a plague nor the consumption of a fecal sac.

At first I thought the chicks barely had the strength to lift their heads, but the more I watch, the more I realize that they control the wobbling—that they bash their siblings out of the way to partake in that life-giving vomit. They are trying to survive. They are trying not to waste away into piles of pink jerky. In the morning, I spread peanut butter on my toast and ponder them. Each of their brains must be the size of a lentil. With a brain like that, I doubt there's any room for sweetness. Hunger must be all that they can feel.

Only the Essentials go outside—those important enough or privileged enough to receive the antibody treatment that allows them to move freely through the world. One hundred and thirty-three days ago, when they first sent me home from the radio station, I thought my livelihood might die. Everything was dying then—the restaurants, nail salons, and sporting events; the movie theaters, flash mobs, and fashion shows; the parks, the swimming pools, and all the people. There were so many people who died.

Instead I started writing more than ever. Now I get ten requests a day—shill this, shill that. Coax forth a pleasing nugget of capitalism in a sixty-second ad. Make the message tighter in thirty seconds. Buy it online. Have it delivered. Whatever it is—it's something you need. "Gruff country voice," I write in the production notes, or "bubbly, feminine delivery."

When I am writing, I cease to be Mariel and I switch back and forth between Mary and Ariel. Mary implies that an air purifier can protect your family from the plague. She insists that you need a push-up bra to feel good about yourself when you've been home alone for several months; she claims that shipping your valuables to an online pawn shop is the smartest way to make your rent. Then Ariel comes in. She couldn't write a good ad to save her life, but she can render a sensational ad less loathsome. Mary the creator. Ariel the Backspace Queen.

I buy everything that Mary and Ariel sell. Why run the risk of missing out when there's nothing else to do? I sit in my office, which is really just a corner of my studio, and while I am writing I ready myself for the sharp beep of a package being scanned. Then I don my mask and rush to the door, but I can never catch the courier. Only the box remains. For a few days I delight in the novelty: a monogrammed eye pillow, gummies that Mary promised would make me thin, an immersion blender, a Hitachi Magic Wand, earrings made from the blue iridescent wing of a Filipino butterfly, fitness leggings, a Cajun spice set, and a blanket designed to look like a tortilla so that I can roll myself up and post a killer selfie using #quarantineburrito.

When I tire of these objects, I throw them in the garbage and then I knot the bag and leave the bag outside of my apartment. I sit in my office until Robbie the maintenance man comes tromping down the hall. Then I don my mask and rush to the door, but I can never catch him before he removes my fecal sac. I suppose that I could wait by the door and thereby guarantee our interaction, but instead I always chicken out. In the early days of the plague, there was no discernible difference between having a body and being a vector of disease. Now they assure us that Essentials aren't infectious, but my own body hasn't quite adapted. I hyperventilate when I think of Robbie— half from excitement, half from the fear.

Robbie is the designated Essential for the whole apartment block. Sometimes I hear him using the industrial vacuum or coordinating with the couriers who bring us food and medicine and other vital purchases. Other than that, I don't know how he spends his time. The rest of the building has a better view. West faces the entrance, North faces the thoroughfare, and East faces the dumpsters. I imagine the residents like iron filings dragged to their windows by the overwhelming magnet of his body. Watching him open the door, walk down the sidewalk, deposit the bag. Whereas I, on the south face, overlook a barren parking lot where nothing stirs except the birds outside my window.

The living things within my sphere of influence are five. I call my mother weeping.

"Is that sweet?" I demand after I detail how the baby ceased to lift its head. For a while the other babies stepped on it and trod it down into the bottom of the nest, but then the mother or the father came, plucked up the body, and tossed it away. "A decomposing nestling might attract a predator," Audubon Online explains to me.

"Oh Mariel," she says. "They're just trying to protect their other babies."

My mother has angled her camera correctly, and I can see her whole head, including her comically uneven bangs. That was our ritual when I was growing up: every month, flush with confidence, she'd wind up butchering my bangs. After the final, fatal snip, when she stepped back to survey her handiwork, she'd always launch into the same soliloquy. "Oh world!" she'd cry. "Why am I me? Why can't I ever find my keys? Why can't I cut my daughter's bangs?"

I am talking to my mom while wrapped in the tortilla blanket—one of the novelties I kept, because I knew that it would make her laugh. I can see myself on camera in a little box at the bottom of the screen. The lower half of my face is covered in tears and snot. I gleam like the glossy finish on a table.

"Oh, shhhhh," my mother says. "It's okay to cry. You're not just crying for a baby bird, you're crying for everyone. You're crying for the world."

But I think I actually *am* just crying for a baby bird, or for some other equally dumb reason. I never want my mom to cut my bangs again, and yet I'm crying because she can't, or because there's too much Mary in me, or because the Filipino butterfly earrings are made from Filipino butterflies. I can't stop crying because I can't start crying for the right things, and that makes me cry even harder. I sop at my face with the edge of the tortilla.

Out the window, I see the three remaining babies. It is their sixth day of living. When the mother finishes her feeding and flies away, the babies lose their energy. They've each been straining upright, trying to be taller than their siblings, but now their heads sink slowly down as if they're already asleep. They collapse into a pile, each neck draped across another. They form an interlocking circle, like some kind of talismanic ordering that is meant to keep them safe.

I watch the mother groom the babies in the nest, parsing their pink flesh and snapping up the white mites that course across their bodies. She vomits up a spider and the tallest, plumpest baby eagerly receives the prize. It swallows the spider, but the long black legs poke out from its mouth like an accidental horror movie—the alien arachnid emerging from the tender body of the baby bird. It gulps and shakes its head to coax the spider down its gullet, but then gives up and collapses back to sleep. It has no sense of menace or impending doom—there's only space for hunger or exhaustion.

When the mother returns, the baby springs awake with the legs still sticking from its mouth. The mother swallow is not gentle—she uses her beak to jam the spider down the baby's throat. I sense a certain level of exasperation. It makes me gag a little just to watch it, though I'm sure my mother would defend the sweetness of the act.

I recall a rumor from my adolescence—how the high school boys, swollen with hormones, their knobbly Adam's apples nearly popping from their necks, devoted themselves to a bizarre masturbatory practice called the Stranger Technique. They would deaden one of their hands by jamming it between their mattress and box-spring, or they'd cover it with a couch cushion and have a buddy sit on that, or fall asleep with their hand beneath their head and wake eight hours later with the throb of morning wood. Then, when they masturbated, their numb hand would feel like it belonged to someone else.

In truth, I am not so interested in using the Stranger Technique for masturbation. I still have my Hitachi Magic Wand, which does a better job than any hand I've ever met—my own or someone else's. But there are other things I want. I practice speaking ads into dictation software while sitting on one of my hands. After an hour, when my hand is suitably numb, it presses my bangs flat like my mother used to do, or pulls down my ear-lobe and stabs an earring through the hole. The stranger pinches me on the shoulder to make sure that I'm paying attention, then traces the sweaty band of flesh beneath my breasts. Once I had a lover who used to touch all my moles in a specific order, as if my body were a bank vault and only he possessed the secret code. Now the stranger inputs sequences that open me. Another man I used to know would rest his hand on the back of my neck when he walked by my side—an act I did not like, because I read it as a signal of possession. Now all I want is for the stranger to steer from the node on the back of my neck, though I have nowhere to be and nothing to do except write these endless ads.

"At Heritage National Bank, we're here for you," dictates Mary. "That's why we're making free self-care webinars available through our online banking portal."

"Here at Heritage, our team of banking professionals briefly considered suspending maintenance fees on accounts that didn't meet the minimum balance," adds Ariel. "But when we say that we're here for you, we don't mean *here for you* here for you. We mean here for you like that scuzzy ex-boyfriend who texts to ask if you're doing okay and then never responds to your answer."

"Stop dictation!" Mary shouts. "Delete word delete word delete word—"

"That's fine," says Ariel. "But can we stop pretending that webinars are the pinnacle of altruism?"

"*Free* webinars," says Mary.

They bicker over what constitutes generosity while numbness builds the stranger up inside of me. Only at the first touch do they quiet themselves—Mary abandoning all her gilded claims, Ariel all her futile protestations. Pinching, caressing, pressing, twisting, slapping, stroking, scratching—I do all of these things. I allow the stranger to reach down my throat with the brusqueness of the mother bird. At other times, when I am sick of being me, I sit on both of my hands. Then, when my numb right hand clasps my numb left hand, I find myself completely nullified. I stare at the words on my screen as the strangers take solace in each other.

When the babies were born, they were tender and pink, covered in sparse puffs of down that somehow made them look more naked. Now, on their twelfth day of living, their skin is black and pricked with feathers. Their mother is no longer the sole trigger for their fits of energy. Sometimes, when she is away, they cheep and fidget in the nest. "Where are you," they cry, "and why have you abandoned us?" This is an evolution. They don't just come alive to eat; they come alive remembering they want to live.

Another milestone: the cessation of the fecal sac. Instead, in their burgeoning maturity, they push their butts over the edge of the nest and streak the side of the apartment building with grayish, gluey shit. I eat my peanut butter toast and ponder this development. Are they hinting at my own next evolution? No more garbage bag for Robbie to collect. I'll toss my newest acquisitions out the window: a decal declaring my support for NPR, a drywall hammer, a candle-making kit, shoe polish, a pink beret, and Boggle. I imagine all the lettered dice lying in the parking lot. But if a word forms with no one to read it, is it really there?

The mother bird isn't bothered by her babies' stream of shit, but my south-facing neighbors are not so easygoing. Maybe they'll call Robbie and tell him that I've lost my mind. Then he'll appear below my window with a garbage bag and a grabby claw. I'll be wearing my cutest clothes, including the push up bra that I haven't yet discarded, and I'll lean out the window and dazzle Robbie with my verbal virtuosity. I'll crack jokes and stun him with the power of my metaphors; I'll make deep observations into the state of the world. I live on the third floor, which is close enough to ground level that he should be able to hear me if I shout really loud through the mask.

Robbie never stood out to me in normal life. He was neither particularly handsome nor particularly gross. He didn't leer at me like the previous maintenance man, but he also couldn't perform MacGyver-type repairs like fixing my leaky sink with a tube sock and a stick of gum. In fact, he made the problem worse and then got soaked and had to call the plumber. But all that doesn't matter anymore. My brief time with the stranger never satisfies my hunger—it only makes me hungrier. It turns each of my pores into a tiny, starving mouth, begging for contact with so much desperation that the fear recedes. He is a passable human; so am I. He has a body; so do I.

"Robbie," I murmur to myself at night, when the mother and the father swallow perch on the edge of the nest with their heads tucked beneath their wings, and all their progeny lie spread out before them, silent and still. But I don't fantasize about having sex with Robbie, I just imagine spooning him in bed. I don't even care which spoon I am, though I used to claim I was a Small Spoon on dating profiles. Now all I want is a body next to mine.

Two days ago, I tossed two objects out my window. The pink beret frisbeed a great distance. The shoe polish fell straight down and smashed itself into a ring of pigment. Alongside the body of the bird that died, they form a strange tableau. I wait and wait, but Robbie never comes. Maybe quarantine has made my neighbors more accepting. Maybe they're not even there. Before the plague arrived, the couple on my left had loud sex on a creaky bed; the degenerate on my right blasted Blink-182; and the grandchildren of the woman down the hall ran noisily up the stairs on Sunday mornings. Now all I hear is the impatient cheeping of the baby birds.

"It was a bad plan to begin with," says Ariel.

"Throw something else," suggests Mary.

Now they bicker all the time. Only the stranger can silence them, but the stranger grows less effective every day. My body has adapted—numb or not, it knows that hand is my mine. I slap myself. It has less sting. I tickle myself on the sensitive spot at the back of my knees, but no longer do I feel the need to laugh. I caress myself—it is my own dull hand, so familiar that it hardly has the strength to stir sensation. When I push the sequence of moles on my body, my body does not open or respond.

I go to my corkboard and take down the business card with Robbie's cell, but when I dial the number, I'm confronted by an automated voice.

"I'm sorry," says the brusque robot lady from Verizon. "The mailbox is full and cannot accept a message at this time. Please try again later. Goodbye!"

I pace down the long hall in my apartment. I use it for exercise, though before the plague I labeled it a waste of space. I ponder the babies. Today is their sixteenth day of living. They've developed rust-colored feathers on their breasts that make them look like honest-to-god

swallows. They're fascinated by the things I've thrown—
they perch on the edge of the nest and squawk frantically at the pink beret, ruffling their feathers, flapping
their wings.

"I think you should prepare yourself—" Ariel begins,
but Mary cuts her off.

"Are you over sixty-two and worried that you won't be
able to maintain your quality of life?" asks Mary. "If so, a
reverse mortgage may be right for you."

Dutifully, I sit down and take dictation.

I inform my mother that the world is full of horrors.

"Yes," she says. "I know."

According to Audubon Online, these include declin-
ing insect populations, habitat loss, cold spells, climate
change, avian lice, predatory bats, cats, and pesticides.

"Mariel, are you okay?" my mother asks.

"I'm outraged," I answer. "They're just gonna let their
babies throw themselves out of the nest."

"It's a natural part of parenting."

"But is that sweet?"

"Of course it is," she answers. "If you care about
your children, you let them go, even when the world is
all fucked up. Like when I dropped you off at college.
Remember that? I put on a brave face when I was helping

you move, but afterwards I parked around the block and sobbed. I didn't want you to know. I wanted you to feel it was okay to go."

"But now I'm trapped in this apartment and I can't come home."

"This too shall pass," she says, but it's only her optimism speaking, and I know it isn't true.

Twenty days after the hatching of the eggs, I get out of bed and find one baby left. Then I fall to my knees and keen.

"No no no," I cry.

The baby cocks its head with quick jerky movements that make it look like it's assessing the situation. But it can't assess anything, because its brain is the size of a lentil. It alternates between peering over the edge of the nest and snapping its beak back in a frenzy of grooming. When it stretches out its sharp gray wing to search for mites, I am amazed—it's like inspecting a newborn's hand and realizing that all the bits and parts and joints are there. The baby looks like a plumper, softer version of its parents. Rust-colored feathers fuzz out around its breast.

"Don't leave," I beg.

"Call your mother," says Ariel. "You know what she'll tell you to do."

"But your phone's too far away," purrs Mary. "Turn your back for one second and the last baby'll leave the nest. And you know what that means—"

Ariel answers with the steady cadence of a well-learned list.

"It grows up. It finds a mate. It builds a nest. Another clutch of eggs. The world goes on."

"No." Mary savors the negation. "It means the parents leave. Momma and Poppa swallow. Abandon the nest. Abandon the baby. Whaddya think? Maybe it'll live another week before it smashes itself into a window or gets exposed to some extra toxic pesticide."

"Appealing to fear," says Ariel. "It can drive sales, but it won't build long-term brand loyalty."

The baby returns to the edge of the nest. Opens its wings. Chirps frantically. Closes them again. Its breast has the perfect roundness of a Christmas bauble.

"Are you stuck at home alone?" muses Mary. "Wondering what gives meaning to your life. No kids? No pets? Ant farm doesn't do it for ya? Can't cuddle a sea monkey? If you're looking for comfort in these unprecedented times, take action today. The future is within your reach."

The baby gazes at the world with such dumb longing. It doesn't understand there's nothing there—there is only this apartment here, the three of us: Mary, Ariel, and me. I open the window. I fold my hand around the baby's body. It's so used to me that it doesn't even flinch. It is very light, very living. According to Audubon Online, a barn swallow weighs the same as three sheets of paper or half a slice of wholegrain bread.

"We'll take care of you forever," I say.

Luz Luz

We should have expected it, but of course we didn't. No one wakes up in their artfully skimpy jammies, yawns, stretches, and expects a sucker punch from God. Six thousand years had passed, and many things got subtracted in that time, most of them mediocre or straight-up bad—slide rules, Skinner boxes, therapeutic leeches, girdles, pellagra, and *Playboy*, to name a few. But for everything taken, two things were added back in—things like GrubHub and Tempur-Pedic mattresses and the revolution in swimming that allowed the breaststroke to evolve into the butterfly. We were happy with our lot. We—the human race, I mean—were like the twenty-somethings who start as minimalists and wind up forty years later owning three hundred thousand household items. It never occurred to us that God was still up there saying "Let there be toaster strudel" and "Let there be semiopaque tights."

Overall, the net effect was Genesis—some things leaving, more things popping up. God hadn't closed the book on creation—the Bible, I mean. He hadn't even finished the first chapter. And then something broke in God, or I guess He just got tired. The most popular theory was that He made all of these discrete and wondrous animals, from blue-tongued skinks to addaxes to black-capped petrels, and then they started disappearing. And you know people. Talk shows where one of the hosts was making sad faces and then planning to fly to Tahoe on her private jet and the other host was questioning the usefulness of God's creation.

"I'm sorry, Mandy, I'm trying to feel sad, I really am, but what have skinks done for *me?* I mean, we're not talking about wolves or bison or whatever."

And I imagine God sitting in his La-Z-Boy and getting pissed. Not a skink appreciator—fine by Me. How 'bout infinity scarves? Shiplap? QR codes? And by the time Kyle the Talk Show Host was missing something that really mattered, it was too late. Because skink is just another word for everything.

So when things started going missing, it was never the animals. Or—let me clarify. Animals did go missing, but we think it had to do with us, not God. The rats and the pigeons stuck around. It was the totoabas we lost, and the viverrids, and the birds that never touch the ground. It was also the pisco sours, the ponchos, those bits of baked cheese that taste better than potato chips, and the towels shaped like triangles that twist around your head.

At first Mandy was upbeat, the way she's paid to be.

"God is just Marie Kondo-ing on a cosmic scale," she insisted. "He's taking back the things that don't bring joy."

And Kyle, he played the cad. "So tankinis disappear? Fine by me. In fact, God, here's a heartfelt plea: take the one pieces, too. You want joy? Turn up the thermostat and leave behind the string bikinis."

Then their faces hardened under all that makeup. String bikinis stuck around, but Kyle wasn't happy. Mandy had to swap the tasteful hoops she always wore for chandeliers, so that she tinkled whenever she shook her head to express her penitence and sorrow. And the people at home, they didn't want banter—they wanted insight into God's state of mind. It turned out that the phrase "God works in mysterious ways" was really only comforting when your thirty-something neighbor died of melanoma, or when toddlers starved in a faraway land.

"He's showing us the sacredness of creation through the horror of destruction," insisted Kyle, who'd made a smooth left turn from playful lech to earnest preacher. "And once we get that concept through our thick dumb heads, he'll reverse the erasures. I'm not saying, like, those tiny measuring tape keychains will return, but the coffee filters, the engagement rings, the external keyboards—he'll give us back the things we need to live."

At first, the sum of my loss was a few empty spots on the shelves at Target. "This item has been discontinued," the signs declared, a formulation that I found comforting, because you could never tell if it was God or just some factory in Malaysia that had gotten caught up in a child labor sting. The same thing had happened a few years ago with a brand of bra that made my breasts look particularly perky; now it was happening again. Was it really any reason to feel hopeless, or to fashion a noose and hang myself from my ceiling fan? No biggie. Genesis and Antigenesis were basically the same.

Every day on their "New News Now" segment, Kyle and Mandy would read off the top Confirmed Missing Items. That way even if you'd never owned a Hungarian goose down duvet or a farmhouse sink, you could still feel a pang of regret.

"Another sad day," Mandy would say.

"I hate to ask. How many?"

"As of one p.m. Pacific Time, thirty-three Confirmed Missing Items."

"Hey, okay, that's sad, but—less than yesterday?"

"We lost forty yesterday. And two weeks ago, the big kahuna—sixty-nine."

And Kyle, who in happier days would never let a sixty-nine go unremarked, would nod his grizzled head with genuine relief.

"Alright," he'd say. "It's tapering off. Mark my words—tomorrow it'll knock down to twenty."

"God I hope so." This was Mandy's cue to shake her head and tinkle.

"Any real standouts today?"

"Corkscrews."

He'd mime sipping from a glass of wine.

"Us winos," he'd say, "will always find a way."

"Until wine goes away."

"Until that calamitous day."

Then one day a true calamity occurred. God was up there engaging in the quotidian extinctions to which we'd grown accustomed. I don't know the exact contents of the list, but I imagine it went something like this:

Unlet the stirrup pants, God said.
Unlet the Ski-Doos.
Unlet the people.
Unlet the strawberry jam.

I was headed to the bank when it happened, clutching a check that I wanted to deposit on the off-chance that checks disappeared. And then—poof. The people disappeared. The homeless man who greeted passersby with a halfhearted mumble, so that you assumed he was asking for money, but you couldn't actually hear any words. The elderly gentleman driving a convertible intended to impress less elderly women. God must have put some kind of safeguard in place, because the convertible just sat there instead of careening off the road and smashing into the Peruvian deli, which now held no Peruvians. Nothing exploded. No one left the gas on. The deli meat spread on the griddle didn't burn. In my hand, one of two hands left on earth, I was holding a check that still existed. It was hard not to feel personally attacked—that seeing how much I valued being a person with money, God simply vanished all the people who gave my money value. I sat down on the sidewalk and buried my face in my arms.

When I got bored of stewing in despair, I sat up and inspected my body. Since all other bodies had disappeared, it seemed that mine must be exceptional. But nothing about me had changed: my right breast remained slightly larger than my left breast. I still had acne scars on my shoulder, soft white down on my arms, and a freckle on the inside of my big toe. In romantic fantasies colored by my obsession with *Law and Order: SVU*, I imagined my heartbroken lover visiting the morgue to identify my burned and mutilated corpse. "It's her!" he would cry. "I recognize that freckle! I know her body better than I know my own!" But I didn't have a lover, though I did have a therapist, some mediocre exes, and a handful of friends. I pulled out my phone and worked my way down the list. The phone rang and rang, but no one answered.

The next step was to inspect the check. It was still in my hand, crumpled and a little damp, because the apocalypse was making my palms sweat. You really can't put anything past God—He once thought a burning bush was the best way to communicate divinity. It didn't seem any more eccentric to pass down the next ten commandments in the memo line of some attractive lady's check. I held it up and squinted. The memo line was blank. The check was signed with a cheerful, loopy signature and made out to my name—Luz Luz.

So there it was—the reason I remained on earth. Except that figuring it out didn't make me feel any better. I just felt lonely in new and terrifying ways. I tucked the check back into my wallet, making sure that none of the corners got folded over on themselves, and then I set out for my apartment. I had driven to the bank, but now the streets were paralyzed with traffic and walking seemed the only way to make it home.

"Dear God," I said, looking up at the watery blue sky, "please consider vanishing the cars, but leaving something usable, like Vespas."

I refrained from adding that I had always dreamed of owning a pink Vespa with a matching helmet. If God wanted to know, He could use His X-ray vision to look into my heart, or to reconstruct the Christmas lists from my frustrated teenage years, when I never got anything I wanted.

As I walked down First Avenue, I kept looking over my shoulder. I'd watched enough horror movies to know the plot: a nubile survivor inspecting an abandoned city, a seemingly peaceful street, and then a horde of zombies flooding down an alley, clicking their teeth to show off their excellent dental work. But the alleys stayed empty; no one came. My only companion was the kinetic sculpture of the hammering man in front of the art museum, a man who hammered at an improbably slow pace, unaware that all industry had ended.

On Pike Street I grabbed a pork bun from a Chinese bakery and sat down facing the big-screen TV on the wall. I recognized the set of the Kyle & Mandy Show, which combined a living room feel with natural accents and Mandy's love of purple. A white sectional sat on a lush white rug, with an ivory fireplace in the background full of lilac-colored candles lofted up on driftwood risers. Mandy had hand-dipped those candles, I remembered, using lengths of purple thread.

At my job as a copywriter for Zulily, I received a wellness credit for attending meditation classes, and whenever the instructor told me to clear my mind, I would instead imagine Kyle and Mandy. Now that they were missing and the TV showed nothing but their pristine set, I felt confirmed in my rebellion. It had all been to prepare for this moment, when I alone could replicate their banter.

"Pretty empty out there, eh," said Kyle, gesturing at the absent audience. Then he gestured at himself and Mandy, and for half a second, their bodies flicked away.

"Confirmed Missing Item: the human race," said Mandy when she reappeared.

"It's a real blindside. I always thought it was us first, then the animals, then all the gadgets and gizmos, and now I find out—we're on the list next to Ski Doos, for God's sake."

"Everyone is gone," said Mandy. Then: tinkle, tinkle, tinkle. Her earrings danced beneath her fried blonde hair. "Everyone except our biggest fan."

"Mandy, you're always better with these foreign stories. Can you explain this one to me?"

"Well, it's a Spanish name—" Mandy checked her notes. "Luz Luz—light twice. It's all just an algorithmic error with the Big Guy in the Sky. She got categorized incorrectly and now she's in this for the long haul."

"Because light comes first."

"Or in this case, light goes last."

"All alone to watch the world end. Sounds like a Luz Luz situation to me."

Mandy groaned.

"Hey, I just remembered—I had this thing for a hippie chick named Sunshine Dusk back in college. I wonder if that gal is still around."

"Kyle, do you need me to explain the gravity of the situation?"

"Given that neither of us exist, I think I get it, thanks."

I vanished the last bit of pork bun the way God had vanished everyone but me. Then I stood, left the bakery, and continued home. A few blocks from my apartment, a murder of crows attacked the walkup window at a pizzeria, pulling glossy pies off aluminum pans and dragging them into the street. A labradoodle loped past, running in the opposite direction. I glanced over my shoulder. Still no zombies. The dog turned a corner and disappeared.

At this point you're probably wondering: Who is this horrible lady, and why doesn't she care more about the world? And by "world" you don't mean all the things, you mean the eight billion people who painlessly entered a state of painless nonexistence. If you're anything like my college boyfriend Tad, perhaps you'd call me vapid—the word he used in a last-ditch effort to extinguish my affection, where before I had fluttered around him like a moth drawn to a dim white bulb. I suppose I was vapid then and I'm vapid now, though it's not like Tad was the great moral compass of his time. And it wasn't like he didn't like things, he just had a different set of references: his Kia Stinger, his Nantucket reds, and the empty bottle of $200 tequila enshrined on top of his fridge.

Besides, how else was I supposed to be? I didn't pick my artfully skimpy jammies because I found them comfortable. Sometimes the shorts got so hiked up that I felt like my vagina was attempting to consume them; sometimes the top, which a fellow copywriter had described as "seductively flowy," twisted around my body like a burial shroud. No—I carefully selected my walnut-colored Lunya washable silk set on the off chance that someone knocked on my door late at night. It didn't matter who it was: a neighbor asking me to turn down the volume on my eighty-inch TV, a stylish woman lost in our apartment block, Tad finally coming to apologize.

In my fantasy, I wasn't afraid of being raped and murdered and winding up on *Law and Order: SVU*. This was the part of the story that happened *before* the events of the episode, when someone actually had to fall in love with me. I would open the door and stand in the doorway, beautiful, attentive, nearly naked in an easygoing manner. Who wouldn't love a woman who looked like that?

Who wouldn't love a woman who rode a pink Vespa with a matching pink helmet?

Naturally, when the people vanished, I had to readjust my expectations. I had to get used to the eeriness of emptiness, the overwhelming silence of the streets. The birds, which I had never noticed before, now raised an unbearable racket, clacketing their delight in life at very early hours in the morning. I missed being able to buy my meals at various cafés across the city—chicken spinach wraps in checkered paper, green smoothies with a gritty texture, bland food whose only real distinction was the ease with which it traveled between Points A and B. I had nowhere to go, no products to describe in great gouts of glowing copy. I rarely smiled anymore, whereas before I'd smiled endlessly so that strangers could admire my good cheer.

But as for loneliness—that was not some new and startling discovery. The new fact of loneliness was not that it existed, but just that it would never go away.

I used Beggin Strips to lure my neighbor's minpin into my apartment. The tag on her collar told me that her name was Gilda, but I preferred Gucci, and the dog didn't seem to care. She vanished on the third day, along with all the cats, ferrets, rodents, reptiles, parrots, guppies, goldfish, etc. I was very sad to see her go.

By the fifteenth day, it became impossible to ignore the growing emptiness of my apartment. I missed my Vivienne Westwood cushions, my Juliska dinnerware set, and other, less illustrious items, like the Audubon Singing Bird Clock that I inherited from my mother and which always terrorized me when the batteries ran low and the birds sang each hour like demented robot jackals.

Cars disappeared on the twenty-first day. I had located my pink Vespa by then, but the discovery was bittersweet—keys had gone missing the week before. I stroked the glossy pink sides of the scooter and left it behind in the shed.

On the twenty-fifth day, mulling Kyle's fling with Sunshine Dusk, I had a revelation. I searched nameberry.com and learned that there might be other names like mine: Zia Zoras, Abner Abners, and Aileen Auroras—not to mention Sunshine Dusk herself. But the only one who seemed to have an online presence was a Zia Zora in Memphis, Tennessee, and her Facebook page didn't inspire me with confidence. For her profile pic, she had a quote from Johnny Depp: "It's not a bad life, just a bad day." She never responded to my friend request.

On the thirty-sixth day, I prepared to hang myself from my ceiling fan. It was Kyle and Mandy who convinced me not to go.

"Buck up, Angel Breath," said Kyle. "When I need a pick-me-up, I go straight for a Jack and Coke."

"Kyle, can you take this seriously for once? Our number one fan—I mean literally our only fan—is about to kill herself, and you're still cracking jokes."

Kyle raised his hands as if to defend himself from Mandy's wrath.

"Look, Lucy Liu, whatever your name is, here's some real advice: when I'm feeling low, I give myself a task I must complete."

I was gobsmacked. I stepped off my wheeled typing table and threw down my jump rope. Kyle and Mandy talked all day long to each other, but this was the first time that they had ever talked to me.

My task: to recreate the set of the Kyle & Mandy Show.

My location: a nearby penthouse suite.

My materials: an ever-dwindling supply of goods.

The penthouse was on the thirty-ninth floor of a luxury apartment building, a property that I had always envied when I passed by on my way to meditation. It would have been an untenable location, if not for the fact that elevators—and therefore the electrical grid—continued chugging along. That was God's way. He didn't let systems go kaput: He kept them working until He vanished them completely. I didn't understand His logic, but then—I didn't understand anything He did. Besides, I couldn't complain. Until the thirty-fifth day, I'd still had access to the internet.

I was no Captain Olivia Benson, but I eventually managed to kick down the penthouse door. It was spartan and white inside, partly due to Antigenesis and partly because the über-rich always circle back to minimalism. They'd opted for an oyster-colored Dresden sectional sofa that I pushed up against their kitchen island. Then, on the island, I laid out a collection of Himalayan salt lamps that I'd culled from neighboring apartments. Lastly, to satisfy Mandy's love of purple, I decorated the set with the purple strands from a beaded curtain.

Then I was done. Then I was tired. I rested my cheek against the couch's modern felt. I rested my feet on the rug that I had fashioned using fluffy white towels from the downstairs spa.

"Day forty-one, and boy do we have a surprise for you," declared Mandy. "Give it up for our newest cohost—Luz Luz!"

"Luz Luz," said Kyle delightedly once the audience had settled down. "It's such an unusual name. Tell us about where it's from."

"Well, it's a pretty common first and last name in Mexico. I never really knew my dad, but he was Raymundo Luz, and my mom just decided she would double up."

"I would never have guessed the Mexican part," said Mandy. "You just look so white."

"Thanks," I replied.

"Before signing on, I hear you were one of our biggest fans," said Kyle. "Like, numero uno."

When he spoke the Spanish words, he sounded like a garbage disposal attempting to pulverize a spoon. But what did I care if Kyle and Mandy were two vapid, ribald, reliably racist, fake-ass capitalist stooges? As Tad could tell you, I had always been the same. I gazed out at the audience. They gazed back adoringly.

"You always kept me company," I said.

"So, Luz," said Kyle, resting his chin in his hand. He had an unusually boxy face, a handsome square rendered smooth by Botox. "Mandy and I, we appreciate the lighter stuff. Dogs doing the electric slide, that sort of thing."

They nodded wistfully, remembering their salad days. Then Mandy leaned forward on the couch.

"But what Kyle is getting at is: sometimes we have to ask the hard-hitting questions. And I have to be honest— we're really struggling with this story of yours. I mean, for most of the time you've had internet, hot water, electricity, everything. Does that really sound like the end of the world? Why aren't you living in a cave? Where's the cannibalism? Where's the photo of your extremely cute kid whose murder you're determined to avenge?"

"I don't have a kid," I said.

They stared back blankly. They looked like two dogs attempting to process a human act that they have never witnessed, like gargling or jumping on a trampoline.

"I think it works better if you understand this as a loneliness story," I explained. "Like the apocalypse as a metaphor for something else."

"Wow," said Kyle. "Mind blown."

As Antigenesis progressed, set design became less about aesthetics and more about whatever I could find. By Day Fifty-Six, I was conversing with Kyle and Mandy while sitting on a pile of horse blankets, which I crawled between when it was time to go to bed. After the kitchen island vanished, I scattered decorative items on the floor. I had a backgammon set for a while, also a Waterpik, a vape pen, a shoe tree, a bag of dog food, a croquet mallet, and one of those dolls that cries when you set it down. I went searching for a replacement item whenever something went missing. Scavenging had gotten easier. Doors had disappeared, as had the element of choice. Now I'd walk into an apartment and find nothing but nickels and a spatula.

On the seventy-fourth day, I gave up counting the days. Time passed. I earned my own segment on the Kyle & Mandy Show. Kyle described it as a way to talk about "all the issues that affect your people." I talked about whatever I wanted. Sometimes, especially when I had secured new items for the set, I spouted ad copy. My job had taught me that it was possible to make anything sound desirable, even a doll that mimicked the worst part of caring for a baby.

My cohosts mattered less and less. Kyle the Lech Who Played at Wisdom, Mandy the Bubbly Maternal Blonde—but I was the one who existed. The audience loved me. Their applause felt as soothing as aloe. I told stories about dresses I had loved and men I had lusted after. I described vacation spots I had seen on Instagram, my experience presenting at CopyCon USA, and the deep vein of inferiority that ran through and informed my life. Occasionally, I talked about my mother.

My mom had a fixation on birds that drove me crazy. She couldn't handle a gas-powered mower or make a passable PB&J, but she could identify a ruby-crowned kinglet by the way it flicked its wings. She was always scattering birdseed in the backyard of the old house and then yelling at the Steller's jays for chasing off the smaller, weaker birds. It didn't matter that the jays were beautiful, with their jet black mohawks and their deep blue bodies. They were everywhere—the Old Navies of the avian world. My mom, like me, loved the Gucci flagship stores.

When she was older and she couldn't get out of bed, she talked even more about birds. I would sit there and pretend to listen, until eventually I had this crazy idea. I became convinced that all our lives could be distilled into a series of photo albums and that we were each allowed to take one of these albums with us when we died. That way when we were bored in heaven, we could flip through the pages and remember the vividness of life. And sitting there listening to my mom rhapsodize about purple finches and dark-eyed juncos, I was certain that instead of "My Beloved Only Child," she would choose the album titled "All the Birds that I Have Seen."

There was another album she sometimes mentioned called "All the Birds I Have Not Seen." It was a much longer book, one tinged with wistfulness instead of triumph. Some birds were rare, some very shy, some existed in other parts of the world, some had gone extinct, and some you could never see because they never touched the ground. You could glimpse them, perhaps, but not *see* *them* see them. You could watch them wheel through the air, but not look them in the eye the way you could when you were staring down a Steller's jay. The one I remember best was the common swift, a bird that had betrayed its name by being driven to extinction.

The swift, when it existed, could spend ten months in the air without ever coming down. Scientists know because they invented tiny avian backpacks to track their movements. This was how they confirmed that swifts do everything on the wing. They slow down and bathe themselves in raindrops. They swoop down and take a gulp of pond water to slake their thirst. They mate in the air, eat in the air, sing in the air. They rest during long ascents, when they fly on autopilot to ten thousand feet, half their brain asleep and one eye open. They weren't made for the earth, except that it's the place where they were born, and this, in the end, was their undoing.

I am telling you, my audience, that soon everything will be gone. This city won't be empty or abandoned, it will burst out of existence like a soap bubble. I have wrapped myself in horse blankets and I am staring out the window. Soon, I believe, the glass will go away. When it is too cold and I am too hungry, maybe God will preserve me like the electrical grid, or maybe I will die. Maybe even stranger things will happen, like the common swift returning to existence and flying to a place it's never flown. Maybe I will join them. My backpack, of course, will be a miniature GG Supreme from Gucci, and in it I will carry the album titled "All the People Who Have Almost Loved Me." Up and up and up I will go, away from all this earthly loneliness. I will fly my way into the much vaster loneliness of the firmament, which God created on the second day. In the twilight of dusk and the twilight of dawn, swifts make their long flight up. For myself, I will choose the dawn, when the sun hovers on the edge of the horizon and the light, my namesake, arrows out to meet the world.

Here I Am

The giant wooden hand in the lobby of the Maven Hotel reminded Ana of the fresco that Michelangelo painted on the ceiling of the Sistine Chapel: God straining to touch Adam, Adam lounging on the barren earth. The spark had not yet passed from the Divine Hand into the Hand of Man—one couldn't ask for too much enthusiasm from a recipient who was not yet technically alive—but Ana still wanted Adam to display a bit of pep, to wriggle like a Golden Retriever at the thought of life. The hand in the lobby, like Adam's hand, simply sat there, hanging open. Michelangelo told his critics, "I am still learning," whereas she wanted to tell her sister, "I hate this bougie hotel."

Ana strode past the pedestaled hand and into the hotel restaurant, a place called the Dawn Room, which featured dangly stainless steel lights and slate-colored walls. The only other customer was a man in a fitted suit dredging his fork through a lake of leftover hollandaise. He smiled at her in the way people smile when they're actually defending their territory. Ana smiled back. She herself was well dressed, a production editor at a successful magazine, but she still felt confident that she could best any Maven customer in hand-to-hand combat, despite credentials that made it seem like she belonged.

A waiter came by to inquire if she wanted to associate her tab with a room number. She did, of course—Pilar, bleeding money, could pay for this—but she didn't know the number and she was explaining the situation when the elevator pinged open and Pilar floated out onto the lobby's marble floor. Her sister was wearing a beige smock that hung past her knees and a pair of slippers made from pieces of durable fabric that velcroed up into a foot-like shape.

"That's her," Ana said.

The waiter eyed her sister's clothing.

"Room number?" he asked, sidling over to Pilar. Ana couldn't hear the answer, but Pilar delivered it beatifically, treating the number like it would someday save his life.

"Late," accused Ana when Pilar sat down across from her.

"I was just getting ready."

"Well you couldn't have been picking your outfit."

"This?" Pilar touched the smock, resting the tips of her fingers on her shoulder. Briefly, lightly, she caressed herself.

"That is ugly."

"It helps with the transition. In order to better let go, one can't be surrounded by things with too much character."

They had not spent much time together in the three years since the accident, the crash of a van carrying a bevy of ten-year-old soccer players. Ana had been there when the doctor said, "I'm sorry, Ms. Araya, but your daughter is essentially dead." And because neither of them had ever changed their names, one married, one not, she had paused for a moment before she determined the direction of the words. What did it mean to be essentially something, but not? Even the Catholics had finally eliminated limbo, pulling the plug so that all those in-betweeners, the unbaptized babies and the pre-Jesus mensches, swirled down the drain towards heaven.

For Lydia, Pilar's daughter, they had also pulled the plug. It had taken forty-eight hours to determine that they could not coax her back. The three of them stood around the bed: Ana, Pilar, and Pilar's husband, Terry. When the doctor came in to perform the second examination, Ana heard him murmur "hot nose sign" to the nurse as he scrolled through the scans on his tablet. For the rest of that night and day and second night of Hell, those words had pricked at her. Amidst the rhythmic hiss of the ventilator, it seemed like the most fixable of problems. She would only need to find an ice machine; to hold chips of ice to her niece's nose till her hands fell numb. Later she learned that it was a secondary sign of brain death. Lydia's brain no longer needed blood, so the blood flowed to her nose instead, a dark triangle in an empty space.

The waiter returned, splashed their mugs with coffee, and scurried back to the refuge of the bar.

"He's scared of me," said Pilar. She poured cream into her coffee so tenderly that it barely seemed to mar the black, as if the liquid had always matched the color of their skin. Norwegian mother, Mexican father. They looked like neither of their parents. Lydia looked like neither of them. Sisterhood was the only visible relationship they carried on their bodies. Pilar was shorter, Ana had a sharper nose, but people always knew. She was willing to bet that even the waiter, so rabbity and inattentive, could tell their story: sisters reuniting before the beige one left behind her human form.

"He knows what you're up to," said Ana.

"People fear what they can't understand."

But that seemed like a dead end to Ana, arguing about what was scary and what was understandable and what was not, and instead she turned to the hotel.

"Could this place be more conceited? When I looked up the directions I saw the tag on their website—'The

Maven Hotel, a haven for maker culture in Portland's city center.'"

"Money's not an issue anymore."

"But 'maker culture,' what is that, even?"

"Make and unmake," murmured Pilar. "I made a child and then she was unmade."

"Pilar, this isn't something to be talked about in public."

"And you can't understand what it's like, not the first step, having a child, not the next step, losing a child, and certainly not the last step—"

"The last step is to unmake yourself?"

"To remake myself."

"And I'm here so you can throw me away? Like all the snazzy clothes you used to wear? Like your job? Like your house? Like your marriage?"

"I'm not throwing you away. But I do need you to do something for me."

"I will not."

"I called Terry last night. He agreed. All my old friends. If Mom were still around, she'd do it, too."

"I will not. I will not make it easier for you to leave your body."

"You can make it harder," said Pilar. "But you can't keep it from happening. Three psychologists have certified my request. I've set a day for the operation."

"What's your timeline?" asked Ana dumbly. It was the kind of question she would have posed to a terrified production intern. It startled her to see her sister's surety. Pilar had always been a reflecting pool of a person—around exuberance, she was exuberant; around shyness, shy. But after the accident her reflective powers ended. Now she projected the ruin of her life, a dim signal of despair that lit the sky but didn't cast light. Pilar made the dark feel more alive.

"Two days. I go in on Friday. And you may not believe it, but I want you to drive me to the hospital and hold my hand in the final moments."

"Careful," said Ana. "You might grow attached to me again. I might hold you back."

"No," said Pilar serenely. "You won't."

The waiter returned. They waved him away. Two cups of coffee—one cut with cream, the other black. She disliked the taste, but she told herself that it was her duty to accept the world without dilution. Last week when the fire alarm sounded in her office, she strode calmly from the building while her co-workers overplayed their agony, smashing their hands against their ears. "You might want to look away," the nurses always said as they swabbed her arm with disinfectant. Instead she made a point to watch. The intensity of her gaze unnerved them—afterwards, tidying up, they avoided her eyes. It was Ana, not the needle, that caused a person in the room to look away.

"I have to get back to work," said Ana.

"Will you do that for me?"

"I have to check my schedule—I have to see if I can move things around—"

"Ana? Will you?

"Let me think."

Ana stood, drained her cup, and walked away. It made her feel weak, looking back, but she looked back anyway. She could see her sister's body wrapped in beige, her sister's limp hair hanging on her shoulders. The wooden hand consumed the space between them. It sat cool and uncomplicated on its pedestal, avoiding existence, not awaiting it. She imagined staining the hand with some type of unapproved cleaning product and condemning its owner for avoiding the messiness of life.

She called her friend Maren later that night and tried to explain how she felt, but she somehow bungled the telling—it was the hotel she described, not her sister, so that afterwards she reflected on the fact that Maren might only have learned to avoid the Maven Hotel. Which wasn't wrong, exactly, but what she wanted to convey was that her sister was trying to pass the spark of life into another body, and that this choice made Ana mad in a way she hadn't felt before, like she wanted to slap Pilar and demand to know if she really understood what it meant to throw away a life. But that version of the story would have startled Maren. It startled Ana, too: how every emotion she felt—love, camaraderie, longing, loneliness, despair—alchemized so easily to anger.

Ana called in sick the next day. The office manager made bland noises of sympathy and healing.

"Feel better," she said as Ana hung up the phone.

But Ana didn't feel better; she felt productive in unusual ways. She pulled on a sweatshirt and a pair of yoga pants, ate from a carton of leftover Chinese, and drove across the city to the Oregon Zoo. It was June. The rain had stopped for what felt like the first time in months and the sun washed everything in tepid warmth. In the parking lot, families flowed around her like jellyfish, amorphous linkages of blood, love, and obligation bonelessly passing her by.

"Just you?" asked the kid in the ticket booth when she stepped up to the window.

"Just me," she answered, and she took her ticket and her color-coded map and walked to the African Safari.

The mole rat exhibit consisted of a single wall painted to resemble the savannah. Words stenciled on the faded, bluish sky announced, "Naked mole rats . . . not your ordinary mammal!" Below ground, in the wash of brown paint meant to represent the soil, glass insets revealed the inner workings of the colony. Mole rats paddled through the tunnels as if the air possessed an extra soupiness. A Zoo Fact informed her that they could run backwards or forwards with equal speed, a piece of trivia that omitted their awkwardness in both directions.

When she'd brought Lydia to the zoo many years ago, Lydia had tried to merge with every animal she saw. She pressed herself up against the glass of the otter exhibit, watching, awestruck, as they ribboned through the water. Ana remembered feeling ashamed of the smudges Lydia left when she stepped back, the imprint of her sticky body on the glass. But it didn't take Ana long to realize that most children experienced this same self-effacing wonder. Adults had a keener sense of boundaries. As an aunt she'd held back. Now, niece-less, she bent so close to the mole rats that she brushed her nose against the glass.

Behind her, a reader board announced in flashing amber letters, "IMPORTANT: THESE MOLE RATS ARE NOT HUMAN." Back in the early days of the operation, she'd overseen a satirical piece in which Photoshopped mole rats carried the markers of celebrity: Frida's eyebrow, Madonna's cone boobs, Sirhana's silver cane. Later, she proofread endless sober editorials about how pain gave meaning to life. But the editorials never stuck with Ana. It was Madonna's mole rat avatar that she remembered, flaunting its pink body in that pointy bra.

The mole rat crisis started after a series of NASA missions demonstrated that long duration space flight was too damaging to the human body—astronauts came back dosed with radiation, their eyes ruined, their bones brittle, their muscles weak. Mole rats, on the other hand, were immune to pain, cancer, extremely low temperatures, lack of oxygen. With implants and special conditioning, they could live for fifty years, and they thrived in tight quarters with their fellow colonists. No other animal possessed this mix of traits; it was as if God had gifted men with dominion of the earth and mole rats with dominion of the universe.

For the better part of a decade, NASA tried splicing together mole rat and human DNA. That project failed, but one team of researchers managed to transfer the contents of a human brain into a mole rat body. The news programs described it as the same process by which a file may be downloaded from one computer and opened on another—an act of lossless compression. The new bodies weren't suited for anything but space—they were tiny, ugly, and functionally blind—but the moles rats could still manipulate buttons with their teeth and communicate via the rodent keyboard. And so the first explorers, a motley collection of human misfits who volunteered to live in mole rat bodies, set out to colonize Mars.

A few weeks later, the mole rat handlers at Mission Control discovered an unexpected side effect. While the human mole rats could express themselves fluently on the rodent keyboard, they had lost the ability to communicate pain. When they experienced trauma in their mole rat bodies, they could not describe the experience, nor could they coherently recall moments of physical or emotional trauma from their human lives. In computer terms, mole rat bodies didn't possess the operating information to run those files. The pain simply sat there, toothless and contained.

Painlessness was a useful quality in space; a priceless quality on earth. Plaintiffs brought case after case demanding access to "therapeutic pain elimination procedures." Eventually, NASA was ordered to disclose the details of the operation. What had started as a special interest story grew into a scourge—family and friends begging their loved ones not to become mole rats, their loved ones becoming mole rats anyway. No major hospitals were willing to risk their reputations on an operation that pissed off everyone except the patient, so private clinics filled the void instead—pain specialists who promised their patients fifty pain-free years at an accredited mole rat sanctuary.

Could Pilar with her glossy black hair and her cream-and-coffee skin truly transform into a mole rat? They were so pink and wrinkled that they looked like their bodies had been papier mâchéd with pieces of prosciutto; their eyes looked like poppy seeds pasted to their skin. Ana straightened, surveyed the room. She wondered who was here to see the funny naked creatures and who was here for graver reasons. To be a mole rat meant possessing a body that could still communicate, but only slowly on the rodent keyboard. It was a body that prohibited all tenderness, except, perhaps, the tenderness that mole rats owed to one another. She could see them snuggled together in the nursery, keeping warm.

Close by, an elderly couple whispered their excitement at finally seeing mole rats in the flesh. She suspected that they had sons and daughters safely ensconced in human bodies. They struck her as the kind of people who watched families fight about the operation on daytime TV. "Give it a try," she wanted to hiss. She'd read on an online forum that the instinct to dig was so embedded in the mole rat body that it overcame the human urge to touch. She imagined the woman holding her husband as he ripped through her hands with his teeth.

The man wore cargo shorts and a button-down plaid; the woman had permed white hair that reminded Ana of her mother. Her mother's name was Linn, but in her later years everyone had called her Cloud, because her hair, thready and thin, formed a nimbus of white around her head. Even the hospice staff had learned to call her that, despite the fact that she was bald as a mole rat as she lay in bed.

For most of her life, Linn loved Juicy Fruit. But the hospice facility had strict rules against gum, and their mother, who was dying from the end stages of esophageal cancer, wasn't able to chew anything. This bothered Pilar—she condemned the fact that the world (what other people called God) could take not just your life, but also everything that made you you, even the brand of gum you'd chewed obsessively for fifty years. Pilar used to buy decks of cards, throw away the cards, and fill the empty boxes with Juicy Fruit. Their mother would take the box, peek inside, and smile slyly back as the attendant bustled around the room changing the bedpan and checking the monitor. Cloud kept all the boxes in her bedside table— sticks of gum stuck in decks of cards stacked like bricks of gold. It was not a scheme that Ana could have invented, because it made no sense—the gum had very little market value and could not be used—but it still made her glad, the dumbness and the tenderness involved in loving other living things.

Ana had never married, though when she was younger she had passed through a series of mostly pleasant men. She had a few acquaintances at the magazine with whom she liked to get drinks, and Maren, of course, her childhood friend who lived in Minnesota with five corgis and a wife. Ana had never considered having a child; Pilar, later, had confirmed that choice. It was like telling the world, "Here is another avenue for ending my life." Ana felt that she had made very prudent choices about who and how much to love, only to discover that the world had stymied her again. Without being able to help herself, she'd loved her father who'd run away, Maren who lived in Minnesota, one particular man who fell in love with another woman, her mother who died, her cat who lived for sixteen happy years, and her niece who became a hot nose. And her sister, of course, the last loved thing—her sister who was throwing her away.

The woman who was not her mother had straightened up after inspecting the mole rat latrine.

"Can you hear them?" she asked the man. He cocked his head and listened. Ana did the same. The woman was right. The room had emptied out and in the stillness she could hear the mole rats chirping.

"I saw a news program about a writer who had a colony in her home, not human mole rats, of course, just animals, and she pushed her desk in front of the colony and she claimed that they would chirp for her when she got stuck," said the woman.

"Did she write about mole rats?" asked the man.

"No," said the woman absently. "I think she wrote about people."

Ana walked out of the mole rat exhibit and wandered through the zoo. In the aviary, a red bird darted through the underbrush. She followed it until the path ended and there was nowhere left to go but back outside. Otters ribboned. Hippos bathed. She sat in the amphitheater during the wildlife show and the hawks swooped low above her head. They moved so fast that she felt sure they were escaping. Then they swooped back, returning to the falconer's gloved hand.

She texted Pilar while she was stopped at a light on her way home.

"Tell me when, I'll pick you up," she wrote.

Pilar responded instantly and without the appropriate level of detail. Four emoji hearts.

The light turned green.

Pilar moseyed up to the car and rapped on Ana's window.

"It's my last chance. Let me drive."

"You can't drive," said Ana. "You're distraught."

"I'm not distraught. You're distraught. Let me drive."

Grumbling, Ana slid over to the passenger side.

"Immaculate as always," said Pilar as she fiddled with the mirrors. "It's like a rental car in here. I remember when we were teens and you would lecture me about how a car is meant to be a vehicle, not a closet or a lockbox or a garbage can."

"Is that really what we're going to talk about right now?"

"It's a good thing," said Pilar. "Blandness makes it easier to leave."

Once, a few months after the accident, when Pilar cut off another car and the long sound of the horn jangled Ana's nerves, Ana had spoken without thinking. "It was someone like you who crashed that van," she said, and then she spent the rest of the drive—the day—her week—her year—her life—regretting it. Now, for the first time in forever, Ana didn't feel like monitoring her sister's driving. She sat back and let the city unfurl before her, one building becoming another, brick and squat, squat and glass, glass and tall. She worked in the district abutting the Maven Hotel, but she still felt lost. No street name or storefront or piece of public art seemed to tell her where she was. The whole city skated by. She closed her eyes. She imagined pushing around a Tonka Truck with her mole rat sister sitting in the cab.

The weather had held for the past few days, that first burst of early summer that caused the whole city to rejoice. The sky hung above their heads like an inverted blue bowl. In the summertime they welcomed their entrapment. Shirtless men played Frisbee in the park and women vogued in short shorts on the sidewalks. Bra straps and spaghetti straps interwove on bare backs and the unhip flip-flopped stickily, their soles unsuctioning each time they lifted their feet. In summer even

Ana emitted a low hum of satisfaction, so that the production interns assumed the role of supplicants—they asked for letters of rec or a few days off for a distant wedding.

"Blandness and release," said Pilar, staring fixedly at a red light. "You just have to say it three times: 'I release you, I release you, I release you.' It's supposed to make it easier for me to leave my body. I wish that you could say those words to me."

The light changed. The car sprung to life. Ana did not answer. They crossed an intersection and then turned into a McDonald's parking lot. Pilar clipped a section of the curb.

"What are you doing?" demanded Ana as Pilar pulled up to the drive-thru.

A tinny voice asked to take their order. Pilar poked her head out the window.

"Yeah, um, give me a plain double burger and—" She stuck her head back in. "Do you want anything?"

"This is so dumb."

"Do you want anything, I asked."

"You're picking this piece of trash as your last meal, really?"

"Just give me the burger," said Pilar, but then Ana leaned across her sister's lap.

"Fries," she shouted. "I want a large fries with that."

The girl at the window handed Pilar their food and Pilar paid and passed the bag to Ana. They drove until they reached the lilac garden at Duniway Park, where they sat in the parking lot with all the lilacs far away.

"Roll down your window," said Pilar. "I want to smell the lilacs one last time." Secretly and ashamedly, Ana liked the smell of fast food better than the smell of flowers. But she obeyed. She was holding the bag in her lap. When they were kids—real kids, before their father left—he would take them through the drive-thru when their mom worked late. If Pilar held the bag she would announce, "I'm going to sample the fries, just to make sure they're hot," and by the time they got home she and Ana would have eaten half. Other times their father gave the bag to Ana. "Hija de acero," he would say, and he was right—she could go forever without breaking.

Sometimes she felt that their whole childhood had revolved around McDonald's. Quarter Pounders when their mom worked late, salads when they were dieting, the drive-thru at 28th and Powell before they put a dog to sleep. She remembered sitting in the back of the station wagon with Pilar and unwrapping the burger like a benediction. No matter how decrepit, how demented, every dog revived enough to scarf it up. "Slow down," Pilar would whisper. They could have lived longer if they ate a little slower, but they never did. Then they would be old again, dragging their long pink tongues across their wet gray chops, and Linn would tell them that it was time to go, partly because of the pain or the whimpering or the tumor the size of a grapefruit, and partly because the living world awaited—jobs, school, book club, swim practice, and anyway, the vet's office was on a busy street and their mother hated paying for the meter.

"Give me my burger," said Pilar impatiently, reaching out.

Here were Ana's choices: she could have tossed the burger into the lilacs, its yellow wrapper lost forever in the purple blooms. She could have lobbed it over the fence and into the tennis courts and then blocked Pilar from entering, or fed it to a dog that some yuppie was walking on his lunch break. But perhaps this would have doomed the dog—the curse by which a plain double hamburger heralds death, even among those who want to live. She could have mashed the burger into her face and eaten it. Or she could have done what she always did—scrunched the bag closed and ignored her sister's pleading as they sat together in the back seat, two young girls.

She reached into the bag, took the burger, and passed it to Pilar. She refused to say the words her sister wanted. But giving—that was different than release.

Then the fries and the grease on her hands and the little tube of salt that she spilled across her lap and the scent of the lilacs hanging in the air. Pilar ate slowly, but her slowness did not matter. The burger vanished. It was time to go. When her sister tried to stuff the wrapper back into the bag, Ana grabbed it and threw it on the ground, because cars were not closets or lockboxes or garbage cans, but perhaps it was fine, on very rare, very sunny days, to sometimes break the rules that ruled one's life.

The Willamette Center for Dolorology was a two-story brick building that reminded Ana of a mid-level English estate. A handful of protesters were clumped around the entrance waving signs that said "Pain gives meaning to life" and "Never again" and "No more mole rats." Pilar led the way, a beacon of beige. Ana walked three steps behind.

"Love yourself!" cried an old man with liver spots dappling his head. He was holding a photo of someone he had lost. The photo was blown up and printed on a sheet of poster paper so that the pixels marred the beauty of the face. A daughter, she guessed—a thirty-something with a scrunchie in her hair, doe-eyed and sad. He must have been speaking to Pilar, but Pilar was walking too quickly, and his words stung Ana instead. She met his eyes.

"Love yourself," he said again, more quietly. She felt sure that he was senile. She and Pilar were wearing the story on their bodies, just like they had at the Maven

Hotel. The beige one rushing towards oblivion and the other, her mirror, holding back. Loving herself wasn't the problem—it was loving her sister that was breaking her heart.

Inside the clinic there was paperwork to complete and a succession of brusque but tender nurses, one of whom shaved Pilar's head. Pilar's hair, straight and black like Ana's, fell heavy to the floor. Her sister changed into a gown, and a transition counselor came in to check that she felt sure in her decision. He administered one final test—a section of financials followed by a section designed to gauge Pilar's emotional state.

Item 7: An estate counselor has reviewed my updated will. Yes / No / Not applicable

Item 10: All dependents have been provided for and assigned a legal guardian. Yes / No / Not applicable

Item 21: On a scale of 1 to 5, I feel encouraged.

Item 22: On a scale of 1 to 5, I feel calm.

He tapped Pilar's answers into a tablet and the tablet tallied her score. He was wearing a short-sleeved button-down shirt, and Ana could tell that he was very fit—one of those young men who wears a spandex unitard and rides a fancy bike. She wondered if he ever thought about being a mole rat, or if he loved his own body too much.

It surprised Ana whenever she recognized her own body-love. It was something she hardly thought about until suddenly it hit her—she felt it when the woman at the salon massaged her scalp while Ana leaned her head back in the sink, or when wine brushed her lips like velvet, or when she sunk her arms up to the elbow in the soapy water meant for washing dishes. There was a quarter on the carpet in her bedroom that she never moved. She liked the thrill when she stepped on it barefoot, how cool it felt as it pressed into her skin.

"Good to go," said the transition counselor, using his finger to sign his name. "Your score falls safely in the eligible range, which means we can proceed with the operation. Before I submit my final report, I just want to prepare you for the first moments after you wake up. Mole rats are a eusocial species, so you'll feel an immediate craving to be among your own kind. We'll get you to the sanctuary as soon as possible, but first we'll do a quick check on the rodent keyboard."

Then he left them alone together for the final time.

"But Pilar," said Ana as they waited, "why can't you hold off for a few more years and become a chimpanzee or a parrot or something more appealing?" The downloading process was specifically designed for human-to-mole-rat transfers, but some of the shadier clinics, especially the unlicensed ones in China, were trying to adapt the operation to different animals. Ana foresaw a new boom in articles. "Ten Reasons Why Macaws Make the Best New

Bodies," followed, inevitably, by the retractions: "Toucan or Toucan't: How Becoming an Exotic Bird Will Hurt Your Family."

"This has nothing to do with bodies," said Pilar. "It has to do with pain."

Ana tried again.

"But how can we be close when you're in such a different body?"

"We were never good at being close in human bodies."

Ana tried again.

"You're leaving me," she said.

"The hurt part of me, not the other parts."

"That's the you part of you."

"No," said Pilar. "Not exactly."

Ana tried again.

"You're hurting me," she said.

"But I'm so hurt," answered Pilar.

A nurse cracked open the door.

"We're ready, Ms. Araya," said the nurse. They both looked up.

Ana tried again.

"I love you," she said.

"I love you," said Pilar.

And in that moment, instead of hugging, they clasped hands. Then Pilar stood and followed the nurse to the operating room. She didn't look back.

In the long interval between being a human and being a mole rat, Ana wandered the clinic. She ate a danish that came out of a vending machine. She listened to people speaking, but she did not speak. In the waiting room, she gazed at the type of glossy magazines she might have made. She thought of the zoo. She thought of the animals, how the happy otters swirled their bodies through the tank.

Finally, after four hours, they paged her on the intercom and called her into the reunion chamber. The transition counselor met her at the door.

"A very successful operation," he informed her. "I've just spoken to the surgeon. Your sister's cognitive files transferred smoothly."

"I want to see her," said Ana.

"Of course."

His dress shoes tapped on the sterile floor as he led her to a table with clear plastic sides about half a foot high. A silicone keyboard was spread out across the center of the table and a mole rat hunkered in the corner, hairless, hideous, and pink.

It was like God had messed up and instead of touching Adam's finger he had touched Adam's toe and the toe had disconnected from the body and burrowed into the dirt. What did it mean to be essentially something, but not? She wasn't sure. She reached out and ran her

finger down the mole rat's bony back. The mole rat—
her sister—gazed up at Ana with sightless eyes.

"They have very sensitive hearing," said the counselor
quietly. "If you announce yourself, she'll know."

"Pilar," said Ana. "It's me."

Letters flashed on the screen as her sister scurried.

Nine steps on the rodent keyboard, counting the space
between words.

"Here I am."

Acknowledgments

Thanks to the following journals in which these stories first appeared: "Ark" in Electric Literature's *Recommended Reading*; "Mothers" in *Hobart*; "Substances: A School Year" in *Craft*; "Is That Sweet?" in *Gold Man Review;* and "Double or Nothing," which was published in *Rougarou* as the winner of their 2021 Fabulism and Speculative Fiction Contest.

Many thanks to all the teachers, throughout all the years, who have helped me reach this point: David Hillis, Steve Duin, Katrina Roberts, Kristiana Kahakauwila, and Kelly Magee.

Thank you to managing editor Carolyn Elerding, marketing manager Bess Whitby, judge Polly Buckingham, and everyone at UNT Press for their careful work to bring this book into being.

A joyous thank you to the wonderful members of the Racoon Rodeo—Abby Feden, Allie Spikes, Hannah Newman, Joey Griffith, John Meyer, Kevin Kohlhauf, and Zack Kaplan-Moss—for reading many drafts of these stories. You are truly my good art friends.

And, finally, thank you to my parents, Michele Ballering and Daniel Arreola, for teaching me to love the world.

Notes

"&"

Dialogue and press release wording adapted from: Kutner, Max, "With an Eye to Mars, NASA Is Testing Its Astronaut Twins," *Smithsonian Magazine*, December 2014.

"Mothers"

Dream images adapted from: Bell, Vaughan, "The Trippy State between Wakefulness and Sleep," *The Atlantic*, April 20, 2016; Brooks, Stephen, ed., *The Oxford Book of Dreams* (Oxford University Press, 2002); "DreamBank," *The Quantitative Study of Dreams* (research website), Adam Schneider and G. William Domhoff, 2022, www. dreambank.net.